THE DEVIL'S DUE

"Don't make me fight you. I will hurt you. You won't like that."

"I don't believe you have the power to hurt me," I replied as firmly as I could.

"No?" Roderick Mellory asked, his voice gently mocking. He pulled me into his arms, very casually. . . . He swung me around, fitting my body against his. He held his face over mine, looking into my eyes. His own were dark and glittering with amusement. His lips curled into that ironic smile, and then they covered my mouth. It had all happened too quickly for me to struggle. After his lips began to move firmly over mine I lost any will even to try to resist him. I would have fallen but for his arms holding me against his body.

He released me abruptly. I staggered for a moment but managed to stand. He laughed quietly. I dared not look at his face again.

"I will send a carriage, Miss Todd," he said, sauntering away with his hands in his pockets. "It will be waiting for you in front in a few minutes. You can go home now."

QUANTITY SALES

INDIVIDUAL SALES

The Master of Phoenix Hall

JENNIFER WILDE
WRITING AS EDWINA MARLOW

A DELL BOOK

Published by
Dell Publishing
a division of
Bantam Doubleday Dell Publishing Group, Inc.
666 Fifth Avenue
New York, New York 10103

ISBN: 0-440-20900-5

Printed in the United States of America

Published simultaneously in Canada

July 1991

10 9 8 7 6 5 4 3 2 1

RAD

1

*I*t had been gloomy all morning. Although the rain had finally stopped, the streets of London were wet and gray. The fog was so thick that the gaslights were burning even now, at barely past three in the afternoon. It was dark inside the dress shop but the frugal Mrs. Clemmons wouldn't let us light any of the lamps. We must conserve oil and save her a few pennies. Everyone was in a foul mood, but no one complained. Our Mrs. Clemmons was a tyrant, quick tempered and hasty to discharge any young woman who displeased her. After three years of this tyranny I was very adept at suffering in silence. I needed the job.

Nan had been going around all day with a long face, her ordinary vivacity smothered by the atmosphere. She was a great one for fortune-tellers and horoscopes. Her simple cockney nature made her easily susceptible to such things. Last week her regular palm reader had predicted a grave di-

saster in the month to come, and Nan felt sure
that today was the day of the dire event. There
were dark shadows about her blue eyes and her
tarnished gold curls hung in tangled clusters. She
sulked in a corner, holding her straw broom idly
and staring down at the bits of bright material
scattered over the floor.

"Something's going to happen," she repeated
for the tenth time.

"Do be quiet, Nan," I replied, rather testily.

"Something's going to happen. I can feel it in
my bones. A black cat was crouching on the win-
dowsill this morning, and I knew then that today
was the day Madame Inez told me about. Black
skies, rain, fog. Something terrible is going to
happen."

"And I know what it'll be if Mrs. Clemmons
comes in and finds you standing there in a daze.
You'll find yourself out in the street without a
job."

"That old bag wouldn't dare dismiss me," Nan
retorted hatefully. "Where would she find another
girl crazy enough to run her errands and sweep
her floor and take in her tea when she has a headache? And all for a handful of pennies. I'm a treasure, and she knows it."

"You're a treasure, all right," I said.

"I'm not smart enough to do anything else,"
Nan said, leaning on the handle of her broom,
"but you, Miss Angel, I can't see why you put up
with this—sittin' here in the dark and puttin' a
hem in a red silk dress for some fine lady to wear
to a ball. Don't you want a red silk dress for yourself?"

"Where would I wear it?"

"Some nice gentleman might take you out."

"There is no gentleman, nice or otherwise."

There was no one. Ever since my parents' deaths three years ago, there had been time for nothing but work. My father, in his quixotic fashion, had left a great many unpaid bills. I had taken it upon myself to pay them all off. Therefore I felt myself lucky to be working at Mrs. Clemmons' establishment and found it was not too difficult to put up with her bad temper and poor wages. At least it was a respectable employment, and that was not easy for a single woman to find in London in this year 1888.

I had a room in a shabby boardinghouse that was nevertheless decent and clean, in a once genteel neighborhood. I had the books my father had left, and I had memories of a spoiled, pampered childhood as the only child of a prosperous middle-class businessman. My father's business folded after some unwise speculations, and his health waned in the months that followed. After his death, my poor mother seemed to lose all incentive to live. She was a shy, retiring woman, living in the shadow of my father's more forceful personality. She wasted away. I was eighteen years old when she died, completely alone, penniless, my only relative a somewhat eccentric aunt who lived in Cornwall.

I managed. I had been managing for three years now. My life was calm and serene. If it lacked excitement, at least there was a certain security in knowing that I had been able to pay all my father's debts. I had even been able to save a small amount. If I sometimes dreamed about a dashing rake who would sweep me off my feet and away from all of this drabness, I had the good sense to know that such things only happen in novels and that life itself is gray, without the flashing colors found in the books I read.

Gray did not suit me. But I lacked the strength of character, the imagination to change things. I was neither happy nor unhappy. Without knowing it, I was waiting. Despite my good sense, I was young enough to believe that the miracle would happen, that some kind fate would see to it that I did not waste away in dust and boredom like the old women I saw at the library when I went to exchange books.

"You should go out more," Nan persisted. "A girl as pretty as you shouldn't have any trouble finding a whole troop of gentlemen. With that lustrous brown hair and those lovely brown eyes—"

"Stop, Nan," I protested. The butcher's apprentice and the printers' devil vied with each other for Nan's affections, only to see her fly off on the arm of a handsome young private in the army. She could not understand why I did not follow her example.

"You may be a well-brought-up young woman," she said, "but that's no reason why you can't have fun. It wouldn't hurt anything for you to let a fellow take you to the Music Hall and buy you a beer."

"Hush," I said.

"You're too prim and proper," she continued. "With that small waist and those nice ankles you should be wearing bright dresses and a piece of lace. No one will ever notice you in those brown and gray things. I know men, Miss Angel."

"And I'm content not to," I retorted. "Can't you leave me alone? I have to finish this frock this afternoon."

I tried not to let Nan get on my nerves. I loved

her dearly. She was such a lively sparrow of a girl, gathering bright bits of ribbon to make her humdrum life bearable. Topsy-turvy and temperamental, she was the only friend I had in the world. She had a tiny room in the attic of the boarding house where I lived, and her adventures and misadventures with all her beaux brought what little excitement I had into my life, however vicarious it might be.

"Finish it," she said, "and then start another, and then another." She put her hands on her hips and stared at me with her head cocked to one side. "You exasperate me sometimes, Miss Angel! Really you do!" She began to sweep up the scraps of material and left me in peace.

The ominous atmosphere outside seemed to creep into the shop. The fog was thick and yellow, swirling in heavy clouds against the windows. There was barely enough light for me to see how to do my stitching. I hoped the fog would let up before Nan and I left. There had been so many attacks in the past few months that it was not safe for women to walk alone in these London streets. Nan grabbed all the newspapers and read the lurid stories of rape and murder with much relish. London was not a pleasant place for a single woman.

There was a roll of thunder. Nan dropped her broom and began to babble again about the fortune-teller's predictions. She stared out the window at the fog and said she hoped O'Connor, the patrolman, would escort us home tonight.

We were both unprepared for the footsteps we heard outside the shop. They were loud, coming down the steps toward the door. The bell made a shrill jangling noise as the door was thrown open, and Nan gasped as the man in a swirling black cape stepped inside. It was most unusual for a man to come into Mrs. Clemmons' establishment, and this one had a hardened face with piercing black eyes that glowered at us beneath diabolical dark brows. For a moment my own heart skipped a beat. I dropped the dress I was working on and got to my feet. Then Mrs. Clemmons came charging in from the back room. She was a fierce old thing with iron-gray curls and the body of an ox. I didn't doubt her ability to handle any situation, and for once I was glad to see her.

The man stood just inside the door. Even if he was not a criminal with murderous intentions as Nan and I had imagined at first, it was evident that he had not come to look at ribbons and bonnets. He stared coldly at Mrs. Clemmons as she adjusted her plum colored skirts and tried to summon some feminine charm before addressing him. Her lace cap was at an awkward angle and her cheeks were flushed red. She wore cascades of jet-black beads and these jangled as she tried to catch her breath.

"Yes, Sir, may I help you?"

Nan snickered at me while our employer fluttered her eyelashes. Her voice was sweet and mincing, hardly the tone she used when scolding her employees.

"Are you Mrs. Catherine Clemmons?" His voice was hoarse, not at all pleasant. It matched his appearance.

"That is correct, Sir. You wanted to see me?"

"Do you have a Miss Angela Todd working for you?"

I drew back, startled. He had come to see me.

"Why—yes. This is Angela." she pointed to me. "Did you wish to see me about her?"

He didn't feel that an answer was necessary. He turned to me, giving me a close scrutiny with those black eyes. He was a very large man, with powerful shoulders, yet now I noticed the soft silver at his temples and the lines of fatigue about the mouth. I could see that what I had thought a formidable demeanor was merely a brusqueness common to many businessmen and his gloves, his neat but well worn suit, the gold watch chain on his vest proclaimed him to be just that, a businessman. What could he want to see me for? I had paid all Father's debts.

"You are Miss Angela Todd?" His voice was softer than before.

I nodded. He looked at me carefully. "Yes, I can see some family resemblance. The same brow, the same proud carriage of the chin." His eyes seemed to grow gentle, and he frowned a little.

"You are related to Mrs. Lucille Dawson of Cornwall?"

"She is my aunt."

"I am Jacob Patterson, Miss Todd. I am a lawyer, and I handled all your aunt's affairs—"

"Handled?" I interrupted. "Why do you use the past tense?"

"I am afraid I have some very bad news for you, Miss Todd."

It had all happened so quickly. I could still not adjust to the fact that my Aunt Lucille had died, leaving me a house in Cornwall and a small annual income. I sat in Mr. Patterson's office now, waiting for him to give me all the details and feeling rather guilty because I was not at the dress shop, putting stitches in a gown for someone else.

Nan had insisted that I buy a new outfit for myself, and I was wearing a dress of sky blue linen and a cape of silver gray rabbit fur, with muff to match. The new clothes felt as strange as the new position.

"You look marvelous!" Nan had cried as she inspected me earlier this morning. "Turn around. Let me see how the skirt hangs—yes, just right. You look elegant, Miss Angel, just elegant. Now things will really happen. Just you wait and see!"

I looked at myself in the full length mirror. The clothes were nice, flattering, but they seemed too bright after my drab gray frocks. I felt as though I were in masquerade as I attached a small bunch of violets on my lapel. The severe, not unpretty face that stared back at me seemed like the face of a stranger. The finely arched brows were delicate, and the dark brown eyes looked too sad and too old. The nose was turned up just a little and the firm pink lips were too large. My only really good feature was the lustrous brown hair, rich with silvery highlights.

"You'll have a fine house all your own," Nan continued, dancing around the room like a child, "and many new dresses and dozens of men coming to call. It'll be a whole new life—for both of us!"

"Both of us?" I inquired.

"A fine lady needs a maid, Miss Angel, and surely you don't think I would let you go all the way to Cornwall all by yourself! Not for a moment!"

She flung her thin arms about me and I was overcome with relief. The thought of moving to a strange part of the country alone had terrified me, but with Nan along it would be much easier.

She was an impetuous, impulsive child, but I loved her.

"What about your gentlemen friends?" I asked teasingly.

"Oh," she said, shrugging her shoulders, "they'll get along. And I hear they grow them big and tall and mean in Cornwall."

"Nan, you're incorrigible."

"But it's such fun, Miss Angel!"

I smiled as she began to make plans. First she would go and tell Mrs. Clemmons a few choice facts about herself and her ancestry, and then she would bid each of her young gentlemen friends goodbye. Then she would buy a new dress for herself, something very gay, and go tell Madame Inez how wrong she had been when she had predicted a disaster.

"She must have looked at the wrong cards," Nan concluded. "I have never known her to be wrong before."

"Do stop babbling, Nan," I said.

I thought about Aunt Lucille as I rode to Mr. Patterson's office. I felt guilty at not being properly sad and downcast, but Aunt Lucille had always been a stranger to me. My mother's sister, she had not taken to my father, so there had been some strain. She had come down to London for my mother's funeral, and after it was over she patted my hand, saying a few words of comfort. I remembered an oddly dressed old woman with flaming red hair that was obviously dyed. As I was her only living relative, she had written a few letters to me during the past few years, but the handwriting was so erratic that I could hardly read them. We had exchanged Christmas cards, and once she sent me a box of herbs that she had grown in her garden.

I knew that her husband, my uncle Fred, had been a gardener at some large estate in Cornwall, and when the master of the estate died he left the Dower House to his faithful servant. I vaguely remembered my mother talking about a law suit. The young heir to the estate had not felt his father had been justified in leaving the Dower House to a servant, and he had tried to get it back, but the Court stood behind the will. My aunt and uncle moved into the house, and after Uncle Fred's death, Aunt Lucille continued to live there alone. Now I, in turn, had inherited it.

The coach moved rapidly over the cobbles, knocking me about, and I clung to the side of the vehicle, peering out at the London streets. I saw run-down old redstone houses with shabby lace curtains at the windows and swarms of dirty children playing on the broad stone steps. A bent old woman hobbled down the block with a basket of rags, and a man was collecting knives and scissors to sharpen on his revolving stone. There were many flowers, even the most humble dwelling having its small patch or a few pots with blooms.

London was loud and congested and dirty, but now that I would soon be leaving it I felt a curious sadness. I would miss the gardens, and I would miss the skating pond in winter and Hyde Park in spring. There was so much color and excitement and history, and I would be trading it all for the bleak coast of Cornwall.

Now, as I sat waiting for Mr. Patterson in his office, I promised myself that I would treat Nan to an outing at Covent Garden before leaving. We would hazard the traffic and confusion and go see an operetta. Nan would enjoy it, and Heaven knew I would miss the theater once I was in Cornwall. Buying the cheapest seats and climbing to the top of the balcony had been something I had cherished over the years.

Mr. Patterson came in, carrying a heavy stack of papers. He wore a frayed but well cut gray suit and there was a blue handkerchief sticking out of his breast pocket. He wore spectacles also, and these gave him a milder look. In the small room his great size was even more evident, and he seemed to lumber about like a caged lion, talking about deeds and other legal documents in very professional terms. I could not begin to follow half of what he was saying, but I sat with what I hoped was an intelligent look on my face and nodded my head when it seemed appropriate to do so.

"You have no desire to sell?" he asked finally.

"Why—no. Not just yet, anyway. I am anxious to see the house."

"The Master of Phoenix Hall would pay handsomely."

"He wants Dower House back?"

"He seems determined to have it."

"I seem to remember something about a law suit he brought against my uncle," I said, hoping Mr. Patterson would tell me something more about it.

"Yes, that was many years ago, and there was much bad blood. He claimed your uncle used trickery to get Bradford Mellory to leave Dower House to him, and there was quite a squabble in court. But the will was airtight, and Dower House was legally your uncle's, as now it is yours."

"What is the place like?" I asked.

"It is small, two floors and a basement, strongly constructed—the finest old stone and oak. There is an herb garden and many trees. One drawback —and you may not like this—the old deserted quarries are right behind the house, fifty yards or so. Could be dangerous if a person wasn't careful."

"Where is it in relation to Phoenix Hall?"

"Half a mile or so, easy walking distance. Not so close you'll feel ill at ease. Your aunt managed to ignore the people at the Hall completely, seldom even saw them on the grounds. You won't be alone, will you, Miss Todd?"

"I shall have a maid. Why do you ask?"

"Well—it's a rugged country. All sorts of unrest."

"Is there—danger?"

"Not really. I didn't mean to alarm you. There's been a lot of smuggling in the county, some highwaymen have been seen on the roads of late. It's a poor county. Phoenix Hall is the only rich estate in the area, and it's gone down since they mined out all the granite."

"My aunt lived alone," I remarked.

"Your aunt was a salty old woman, Miss Todd. She kept a pistol and she knew how to use it. And she was loved by the people of the county. I have mentioned the herb garden? She made poultices and medicines for the neighborhood people and was something of a midwife. People came to her when they had aches and pains, and usually she cured them. No one would have harmed her. As her relative, you'll be in good standing before you even arrive."

He gave me some papers to sign and I signed

where he pointed. I held the quill between nervous fingers and the ink splattered. He blotted it with a piece of felt and waved the deed in front of the window to dry it. He tied up a stack of papers with a ribbon and asked me if I wanted a box at the bank. He agreed to handle all my legal matters for me, and I felt they were in good hands.

"There is quite a bit of money," he said. "Most of it invested. I will send you the statements. You'll get a modest sum four times a year. That's the interest. The rest will still be at the bank, making more." He paused, obviously wanting to ask me a question.

"Yes?" I said, prompting him.

"Have you any knowledge of your aunt's source of income?"

"None whatsoever."

"None of my affair really. I know she was paid well by the people, and she had a brisk business in herbs. I wouldn't have thought it would pay so well—but perhaps she had another source of income we didn't know about." He grinned. "Perhaps a little distillery. I wouldn't have put it past her."

I shifted the muff in my lap. "As you know, my aunt was a complete stranger to me."

He nodded. "You would have liked her, Miss Todd."

I stood up to go. Jacob Patterson rubbed his hands together, relieved to have another successful transaction behind him. I liked the man enormously, and I was sure that he was both honest and efficient.

"You are a lucky young woman, Miss Todd."

"I know. This has all happened so quickly, I can hardly believe it even now. It is like a dream—a place of my own, an income, after years of making do. I feel like a child under a Christmas tree with a gorgeously wrapped gold and silver box just for me."

Jacob Patterson chuckled. He glanced at his watch.

"I must not keep you," I said, "I know you are busy. But, before I go, could you tell me a little about Phoenix Hall and its masters? I am very curious."

"I've never been inside the place," he said, "but I have seen it from outside. It is a vast, rambling place, a huge old pile of stone without any real claim to beauty. It's a mixture of styles, originally built during the reign of Elizabeth and one of the places she visited. It was partially destroyed during Cromwell, much of it burned. It was reconstructed during the next century. Thus it got its new name, rising like the legendary bird out of the ashes. Reborn, so to speak. The Mellorys inherited it during the seventeen hundreds. It has belonged to them ever since. There was coal once, but the supply soon ran out and the old mines were boarded up. There was a large deposit of granite discovered and Bradford Mellory's father quarried it. Bradford Mellory kept the quarries running, even when they had ceased to be profitable to Phoenix Hall, so that his people would have employment."

"He must have been a kind man," I remarked.

"Bradford Mellory was an easygoing, genteel old fellow, it would seem, well loved by all the people in the neighborhood. Phoenix Hall was open to everyone, and he gave grand, lavish parties for the people, the poor folks as well as the gentry. When he died there was much grieving.

The new master is not at all like his father. Quite the opposite."

I very much wanted to hear about the man who was determined to have Dower House back. Jacob Patterson described him to me as a young man just turned thirty, something of a rake and despised by the people. He had been thrown out of Oxford for gambling, and there had been a lot of trouble with the young women of the neighborhood. The first thing he did when his father died was to close the granite quarries, thus putting all the people who had worked there out of work. There had been threats of a riot among the peasants and the troops had been called in. Violence did not break out, but there was still a smoldering resentment for the present Master of Phoenix Hall.

"He must be very unpleasant," I remarked.

"Arrogant, spoiled, tyrannical," Jacob Patterson said.

"Who else lives in Phoenix Hall?"

"His younger brother, Paul. The lad was injured as a child and he is a semi-invalid, interested mostly in his music and books."

"How old is Paul Mellory?" I asked.

"Twenty-three or four, I would guess," he replied. "I have never seen him, but I understand that he is a gentle boy, much like his father in nature and at odds with his brother. There is a sister, too, Laurel. She would be about your age, a pale, pretty lass who tries to make up for her brother's harshness by her charity. The people love her, and the love is well earned. She was a friend of your aunt's. You will no doubt meet Miss Laurel."

"I shall look forward to it," I told him.

I left the office with my head reeling, trying to sort out all the facts I had learned. It was one of those rare, sun-spangled days that can turn London into the most beautiful city in the world, and I decided to walk for a while. The air was fresh and sparkling with a clear blue haze. The sun made silver sunbursts on the windows of shops and glittered on the cobbles. I lingered at a book stall, turning over the old second-hand volumes, finding it hard to realize that I could buy all the books I wanted now. I wandered on, pausing to watch a group of swarthy, muscular men in front of a music store moving a large piano down a flight of stairs while its owner, a small Italian music teacher, made violent gestures and cried encouragement.

The sights and sounds and smells of London were fascinating, and I would soon be leaving them. A vendor stood behind his cart, selling hot bacon rolls, soft strips of bread wrapped around bacon and mustard. He swirled a piece of brown paper around one and gave it to me, and I bit into the delicious treat, feeling like a child on holiday. Small children were gathered around a Punch and Judy show at the next corner, crying out in excitement as the colorful puppets danced on the tiny stage. I stood beside a little girl in a blue dress and watched the show with almost as much pleasure as the children.

Life had been hard during the past few years, and I had been as patient as it was possible to be, waiting for that change that I knew would come, despite my rather grim, realistic outlook. Now it had arrived, and I felt like a new person. Before, I had felt old and weary; I was twenty-one years old, but I might as well have been forty-one. Now

I felt as young as these children and lighthearted. A whole new life was opening up for me, like a flower whose petals had been tightly closed, and I was not going to let Phoenix Hall or any of the people there cast a shadow over it.

2

*I*t seemed that we had been riding for days. The coach was uncomfortable and crowded. Although Nan and I were the only passengers, there were a great many boxes that kept tumbling onto the floor. Nan had brought along her canary, a bright yellow bird with a little golden beak, perched disconsolately on the swing of its small gilded cage. His feathers dropped, as though he too was finding the trip unbearable. The horses galloped over the rough highway, and the wheels jogged over huge rocks, causing the whole coach to rock sideways. We could hear the driver curse occasionally and the sharp slash of his whip as he urged the horses on. Even though the windows were closed the dust was thick inside the coach. The vehicle smelled of sweat and old leather.

"How much longer will it be before we reach the inn?" Nan cried.

"Surely not much longer," I replied.

The coach jogged violently and we were both thrown forward.

"I don't know if I can endure much more," she protested.

"Patience, Nan."

"We've been riding so long!"

"I know."

"I think the driver must be mad, going at this speed."

"He is anxious to get to the inn, too," I informed her.

The last rays of the sun touched the sky with crimson, and it would soon be dark. Through the window I watched long stretches of rolling hills covered with dead brown grass, huge gray rocks rising up in fantastic shapes surrounded by gnarled black trees. It looked ominous and forbidding. It was completely alien to anything I had ever seen before, and I shivered when I thought about those lonely deserted stretches.

Nan spoke comforting words to her canary and made a face at him. It was comforting to have her along, for despite her pretended anguish she was finding this a great adventure. Her face was lit up with excitement. Her golden curls were held back by a small blue bonnet, a sprig of purple velvet clustered about the brim. She wore a new dress of lilac colored linen with many rustling blue and violet petticoats. I had never seen her look so charming with her flushed cheeks and the tiny golden brown freckles scattered across her nose.

"Just think," she said, "tomorrow we will be in our own house. I am sure it will be in a shambles. We'll have to spend a week cleaning."

"I hope there is enough linen," I said.

"I brought along several cakes of lye soap," Nan

said, "and some of that strong polish Mrs. Clemmons used. I hope she doesn't miss it."

"Nan, did you steal it!"

"And this bonnet, too. Isn't it delightful?"

"Anything else?"

"Only some stockings"—she hesitated—"and a lavender silk parasol with an ebony handle."

"Nan," I scolded, only half in earnest, "you should be ashamed."

"The old crow owed it to me after all those years of sweeping up after her and takin' her tea when she'd had a drop too much. We will never have to set foot in the shop again. Never have to hear her roaring when a customer hasn't been satisfied."

"It is well behind us," I agreed.

"I wonder what is ahead," Nan said, reflecting.

"Something wonderful, I hope."

"I am anxious to see the Master of Phoenix Hall," Nan said. I had told her everything I knew about Phoenix Hall and its inhabitants. Nan's curiosity about them knew no bounds, and while I tried to be more nonchalant, I too wanted to know all I could about that fascinating family who would soon be my neighbors.

"I don't imagine there will be an occasion for you to meet him," I said primly.

"What a shame, after all I've read about him in the papers."

"What have you read?" I asked, trying not to sound too anxious.

"Surely you remember all those stories in the tabloids, Miss Angel. They were scandalous!"

"I never read the tabloids, you know that."

"I know—you miss so much. You're always

reading those dreary old books by Mr. Dickens and missing all the juicy things."

"What did the papers say about Roderick Mellory?" I asked.

"I can't remember too well. It's been some time ago. But one story told about a duel he had with an officer in the East India Company. They were fighting over the favors of a music hall actress and they met early one morning in Hyde Park and exchanged shots. The officer got a bullet in the shoulder, and he would have got one in the head as well if the seconds hadn't restrained Mr. Mellory. There was a big write up, police called in and everything."

"The papers always exaggerate those things," I said.

"And there was the time Lord Fitzhubert found Roderick Mellory with the lord's young wife in a private box at the Ascot Races. Lord Fitzhubert slashed Mr. Mellory across the face with a riding crop. It seems that Mr. Mellory had been seeing young Lady Fitzhubert privately on many occasions. She's a lovely blonde thing, they say, always wearing her pearls and lots of pink silk."

"Gossip," I said, intrigued in spite of myself.

Before leaving London I had seen Mr. Patterson again. He had a list of instructions to give me and more papers for me to sign concerning some investments he wanted to make. I had pressed him for more information about the Mellorys and he told me that Roderick Mellory was trying to put the estate back in order. It had lost considerable sums since his father died, and the new master of Phoenix Hall had spent three years in India, occupation unspecific, earning money to spend on the estate. He had recouped most of the losses, invested the money with the Bank of England, and only recently had started making repairs on the house. Getting back Dower House seemed to be an obsession with him, and Patterson had received another inquiry about the purchase of it since the first day I was in his office.

He had also told me something more about Laurel Mellory. Her mother had brought her to London for The Season and the young debutante had been presented at Court. She had been squired about at all the balls and parties and had gone to all the fashionable places, yet it had been a failure for the most part and mother and daughter had gone back to Cornwall, disillusioned with London society. Young Laurel was evidently more interested in her good deeds, her young brother, and the gardens than in finding a suitably wealthy husband. Mrs. Mellory had died two years later with her daughter still unwed.

I was interested in them all: the Master with his violent disposition, the pale young girl who had been a failure in London, the gentle boy with his lame leg and love of music. My new neighbors might prove to be antisocial, but they would certainly never be dull.

All the light had washed out of the sky now and heavy shadows veiled the horizon. The coach lurched and shook. I felt my eyelids growing heavy, and my head nodded. Nan was already asleep, curled up in the corner on her side of the coach, the canary's cage in her lap, her arm curved about it protectively.

A box tumbling to the floor awoke me. It fell with a crash, and I sat up with a start, my eyes wide open. If the coach had been going fast before, it was fairly flying now, crashing over the road at a pace that seemed impossible. Nan and I were like rag dolls caught in a box being tossed up and down by some demonical child. Nan let out a shrill scream as a pile of boxes tumbled over her. I gripped the leather strap by the window, trying to catch my breath.

The air around us seemed to be full of explosions. It sounded like Trafalgar Square on Guy Fawkes night, firecrackers bursting. What we heard was the driver's whip slashing the air violently, rocks flying up to crash against the side of the coach and tree limbs that scratched it. There were shouts, too, from more than one throat. Nan was quite plainly terrified, and my heart felt as though it were going to leap into my throat.

"God in Heaven!" Nan screamed, her blue eyes twice their normal size. "What is it!"

There was an ear-splitting explosion and I saw a flash of flame. It was followed by the splintering of wood. The coach almost toppled over, but somehow the driver managed to hold it on the road. There could be no doubt now. We were being pursued by highwaymen.

"Guns!" Nan yelled. "Murder! Lord preserve us!"

I saw a dark figure streak past the window. It seemed that we were surrounded by horses. There was a final great lurch, the screeching of wheels and a jolt as the coach came to a stop. There was a sudden silence and Nan and I stared at each other. My heart was still beating, but I was not nearly as frightened as I had been when the coach threatened to go off the road and crush us as it rolled over. Nan sat up, adjusting her skirt and retrieving her bird cage from the floor. Her bonnet had fallen off and her golden curls were scattered chaotically over her head. There was a large streak of dirt across her cheek. She peered out the window with curious eyes.

"Keep still, Nan," I warned.

"We're surrounded," she whispered excitedly.

We heard loud voices and the sound of the driver climbing down from his seat. A lantern was lit and held up. We saw a group of shadowy figures in the flickering yellow glow. The door was jerked open and a hoarse voice commanded us to get out. I moved slowly, stepping out carefully. A hand seized my arm and pulled me into the open. Nan fairly leaped out of the coach, clutching the canary's cage. The bird, for some strange reason, was chirping a bright, monotonous song.

"Just keep quiet, Ladies," a voice directed, "and you will not get hurt." The voice was hoarse and gutteral, but it was obviously not natural. The man was disguising his normal speaking voice, and rather poorly, I thought.

There were three men, but the man with the forced voice was obviously the leader. He was very tall, powerfully built, and dressed entirely in black: highly polished black leather boots, tight black pants, black coat. There was a silky black hood over his head, with holes cut at eye level to enable him to see. On top of that he wore a broad-brimmed black hat, similar to those affected by the cowboys in America. The other men were burly brutes in leather jerkins and dusty trousers, bandanas tied over the lower part of their faces. One of them held the lantern.

"Who are you?" Nan cried.

"No questions, young woman."

"Don't you touch us. Don't you dare."

"Shut up, Nan," I hissed.

"Take your friend's advice," the man in black told her.

"You don't frighten me," she snapped.

"No?"

He moved toward her slowly, menace in every step. He raised his black-gloved hand as though to strike her, and Nan stood there without flinching, her chin thrust forward arrogantly. She was a ludicrous figure in her lilac dress, holding the bird cage tightly, the smear of dirt across her face. I took her wrist and jerked her beside me, putting my arm about her waist. I had to admire her for this outburst of courage, and somehow I got the impression that the bandit did, too. We both stared up at him, and he watched us for a moment, his head held to one side as though he were making a decision. Then he chuckled.

"Brazen pair," he remarked to his companions. "Most of the women scream or faint or both."

He stepped over to me, peering closely into my face. I could feel his eyes examining me.

"What about you?" he asked. "Are you going to faint?"

"I don't think so," I replied calmly.

"All calm and collected. Cool. Well bred."

"Would you prefer us to scream? Do you enjoy intimidating women?"

He chuckled again, nodding his head. "Spirit, too," he said to the others. "I like that."

Our driver was leaning against the coach, his face pale and his chest heaving. One of the men held a long pistol aimed at the driver's head, and the poor man was much more terrified than either Nan or I. He was still panting from the exertion of the chase. The horses were standing quietly in their traces, their coats gleaming wetly in the light. I saw a large splinter near the top of the coach where the bullet had gone in.

"What do you want of us?" I asked.

"Of you, nothing," the man said. His voice was more normal now. I caught a cultivated accent that bespoke of education. This man was not a peasant. He carried himself too well. Even clothed all in black as he was, there was an unmistakable elegance about him.

"We have no valuables!" Nan snapped.

"Indeed you do," he said with a tone that was very low, "but I am afraid we don't have time for that."

I blanched. Nan called him a highly unflattering name. He laughed. The other men stood as silent as dolts.

"We are not going to harm you," he said. "All we want is that box tied to the top of the coach. You" —he turned to driver—"get it for me."

"You can't take that box!" the driver cried, suddenly finding his voice. "It belongs to the government!"

The man moved very slowly. He stood in front of the driver, who cowered against the coach, his eyes rolling in fear. Quickly, almost too quickly for the eye to follow, the black gloved hand slammed across the driver's face, then again, making two sharp, loud explosions as leather met skin with impact. The driver gasped. In the dim yellow light I could see his Adam's apple bobbing.

"Next time it will be with the butt of a pistol," the man said quietly. "Now get me that box."

The driver clambered up to the top of the coach and unfastened the small metal box that had been secured there with some of our luggage. I watched his shoulders fall dejectedly as he tossed the box down at the feet of the man in black. The box split open. Several gold pieces rolled about our feet. The two silent brutes began to gather it all up quickly. The man in black stood watching them.

"Government funds," the driver said. "You'll pay for this, just wait. You'll get caught."

"Shut up, you." His voice was low but much more deadly than it would have been had he yelled.

The driver was suddenly brave, or perhaps just uncaring. "How did you know it was coming by passenger coach, instead of the regular way? How could you possibly have known it was on this coach?"

The man did not reply. His men had gathered up all the money, and they put it in one of the saddle bags. They climbed onto their horses, waiting patiently for their leader. He turned to Nan and me, making a formal bow and taking off his hat.

"Charmed," he said. "I would have liked to meet you under more pleasant circumstances—" He hesitated. "Perhaps I shall yet. I hope you have a pleasant journey, Ladies."

He swung onto his horse and we heard them galloping away. It was very quiet. They had blown out the lantern and only the frosty light of the stars gave illumination to the scene. Then a cricket began a chirp and another followed suit. The night air was chill. But I felt a much stronger chill inside of me. It was not caused by the night air. It was caused by the tall, powerfully built man in black with a face covered with black hood and the voice and manners of a gentleman.

* * *

The inn was rustic and very clean. I had a small room on the second floor and Nan's was right next door. Both of us had bathed, and I stood at a mirror now, brushing my long brown hair. A candle was burning in its pewter candlestick, casting a warm orange light over the room. It had dull gray walls and a white ceiling. The furniture was plain, and the only touch of color was the large, brightly hued rug on the floor. After riding in the coach all day, the room seemed like unparalleled luxury to me. There was the tangy odor of an apple that someone had left behind, and the breeze, swelling the stiffly starched white curtains, brought in all the smells of the night. It seemed incredible that the highwaymen's holdup had taken place only two hours ago.

Although I had been exhausted before, now I was vividly awake and all of the tiredness had vanished. The hot bath had refreshed me, and the excitement had stimulated me. It was not yet midnight, and the mistress of the inn was preparing a late supper for us. I did not think it would ever be possible for me to sleep.

Nan came into the room, looking fresh in a faded pink cotton dress. It had a wide white sash and there was a white ribbon in her hair. She was aglow with excitement. Nan had never been outside London before, and this was all very thrilling to her. She was a strong, sturdy girl, had taught herself to read and write by sheer willpower, and she was prepared amply for any adventure that might occur. A mere holdup could not greatly disturb her.

"Let me finish brushing your hair," she said.

I handed her the brush and sat down before the mirror.

Nan began to brush my hair with firm, gentle strokes. I closed my eyes and relaxed. Nan would have waited on me hand and foot if I allowed her to. Servitude was in her nature. Her mother had been a washwoman, and her mother's mother had been an indentured servant.

"I wasn't a bit afraid." She had talked of nothing but the holdup. She fancied herself something of a heroine and tended to exaggerate her bravery. I could see the story growing in her mind. In retelling it to a stranger she would no doubt add dramatic embellishments.

"You were very brave," I agreed.

"That's the first time I've ever seen a bandit close up, although I saw a pickpocket in Piccadilly one time. Do you think he will get away?"

"I have no idea."

"The stable boy—I talked to him while you came on upstairs—told me this black highwayman has been operating in this part of the country a long time, almost two years. They haven't been able to trap him. He has a secret hideout where he keeps his loot, and he only goes out three or four times a year, when there is a large amount of money being sent. He must be a clever devil."

It all sounded fantastic to me, too much like an adventure tale. In the clean, calm room with the soft candlelight, it seemed hard to believe that it had actually happened.

"He's not an ordinary bandit," Nan continued. "The boy says he's a resident of these parts, probably very respectable, with access to information about the money shipments. That makes it all the more exciting, don't you think, Miss Angel?"

"They'll catch him, Nan. Without your help," I added.

"I'd like to be there when they take his hood off."

"Stop prattling," I said. "We must hurry. The meal will be cold."

She laid the brush aside and arranged my hair, fastening it with my silver hairpins.

I was wearing a blue and brown checked dress with a dark brown bodice. The long skirts rustled as I moved across the room. We went down the narrow wooden staircase and stepped into the warm atmosphere of the public room. It was very large, with dull red walls and sawdust over the rough stone floor. A fire was roaring in the large stone fireplace, and the flames cast reflections on the copper pots and pans that hung on the walls. Rough wooden tables and chairs were arranged comfortably. There was the smell of hot sausage and the not unpleasing odor of stale beer.

The mistress brought up hot rolls and sausage and a dish of hashed potatoes. Like everyone else, she had been excited by the holdup, and she lingered at our table while Nan related for the tenth time what had happened, adding the expected embellishments. The woman's brown eyes grew large and Nan told of her defiance of the bandit. She called Nan a brave girl and patted her hand before leaving the table.

The driver was sitting at a table in the corner, surrounded by a group of men who were talking quietly. A local constable had already arrived and he came over to our table and asked us to make statements. We told him what had taken place and he listened gravely. The mistress came in with an apple pie and thick cream. We finished our meal in silence, both of us beginning to grow a little weary after the hot food. I was ready to go back to my room when the innkeeper approached us.

"You're a brave pair," he said, putting his beefy hands on his hips. He wore a leather apron and his sleeves were rolled up. He had a typically peasant face, large, open, weathered, with strong features. Honesty was apparent in every line.

"Going to the coast?" he asked.

"Yes, near Penzance," I replied.

"Rough weather there," he said, "rough country for two young women alone. Going to join your family, Miss?" His questions were not rude. They were merely the questions of a simple, straightforward man who was genuinely interested. This was a lonely part of the country. I could understand why he liked to talk to anyone who stopped at his inn. I told him our exact destination and that I had inherited a house there on the Mellory estate.

"The Mellorys of Phoenix Hall?" he asked.

I nodded. His eyes grew dark with concern.

"The worst spot in Cornwall," he told me. "I fancy you won't be staying there too long, Miss. It's a rowdy county, and there is much dislike for those Mellorys—at least for the Master. He closed down the granite quarries and put a lot of people out of work. I wouldn't be anywhere near Phoenix Hall, not on your life."

Much later, as the pale moonlight poured into my room, I thought about his words. Did no one have a good word for Phoenix Hall? Could Roderick Mellory, a man I had never seen, really be all that bad? Was this part of the country completely wild, with highwaymen and tensions and unrest among the common people? I had heard about the fierce coastal storms and the destructive gales, and I imagined that the emotional climate was equally fierce. I tossed restlessly between the coarse, heavy linen sheets. They had been freshly washed and smelled of strong soap. I tried to sleep, but it was impossible.

I felt I was in a state of suspension. London, and my life there for the past twenty-one years, was behind me, and ahead there was only the unknown. We would reach the village tomorrow at noon, and shortly thereafter I would be in Dower House, my new home. I wondered what awaited me there. I finally slept, and I dreamed wild, stormy dreams that might have been a prediction of what was going to take place soon.

3

*T*he air was glorious, strongly laced with salt, and even though we had not yet seen the sea there was the unmistakable sense of its nearness. I could feel it, an almost human presence over all the countryside. The coach was making a slow winding climb up a hill, through pine trees and scrubby oaks with blackish-green and rusty brown leaves. As we reached the top of the hill we saw the ocean for the first time, a surging blue-gray mass with a life all its own, moving out to a misty horizon. Dunes covered with the stubble of salt grass slanted down to the water and sea gulls circled aimlessly. I felt my heart leap with excitement as I saw this beauty unlike any I had ever seen before.

"It's marvelous, Nan," I exclaimed.

"Pretty," she said, more restrained in her admiration.

"Look at the water—and the gulls. The sun on their wings."

"Nice," she agreed.

Up in the distance a town was set on some rocky cliffs, and near at hand there was a sprinkling of farms and fishermen's houses. They looked rough and raw, beaten by the sea wind, but their colors were bright in the harsh white sunlight. Plumes of smoke rose from the chimneys, and I saw tiny figures moving like toys. This was a Cornwall sunbleached and peaceful, surely no place for violence.

We rode along the ridge for a long time, passing many small towns, as lovely as the first, before turning inland into a heavily wooded area. It was cooler here in the shadows of the trees with pine needles making a soft floor for the wheels of the coach. We passed a man leading four cows with a long stick. He prodded them over to the side of the road and they stood watching with placid bovine faces as the coach joggled past. Later on I saw a little girl with bare feet, her yellow hair the color of straw, walking along the side of the road, surrounded by geese who honked loudly as she scattered bits of grain before her. Nestled in her arms was a tiny brown rabbit.

"It looks so peaceful," I told Nan. "I think I shall love it."

I meant it. I had never seen the country, my life having been confined to the city. This was a new world unfolding, and I found it enchanting. My whole body seemed to be tingling, as though my blood had been revitalized by the salt air and the fresh, sharp breezes. I leaned out the window, taking in everything with hungry eyes. The experiences of the night before, the highwayman, my chill, my apprehensions had all been temporarily forgotten.

Four sturdy young men crossed the road, carrying farming implements on their shoulders. They were talking loudly and joking like all healthy young men. They stopped to watch the coach pass by, and one of them let out a raucous yell when he saw Nan perched forward with her golden curls clustered about her face. She waved to the men and settled back onto her seat with a sigh. After that she began to show a little more enthusiasm. As long as there was an ample supply of fine looking men, Nan could be happy anywhere.

The coach finally reached Lockwood Village and we alighted. It was larger and greener and more congested than those villages directly on the coast. Most of the people earn their living working on small farms, but some of the men traveled thirty miles each day to work in the coal mines. The closing of the Mellory quarry had been a great blow to the local industry, but these people were strong, resilient, most of them living all their lives in this one spot, and they had the ability to make the best of what they had. If there was not wealth, there was fresh air, plenty of exercise and an abundance of milk and eggs and farm products. These gave the villagers a ruddy, healthy glow that I had never seen in London.

The driver set our luggage on the platform in front of the station, then he went off to find someone who would drive us to Dower House. I stood under the shade of the awning and looked at the village. There was a square with a weathered marble monument surrounded by newly green grass. Several ancient wagons were drawn up around the square and men were loading produce onto them. A group of shabbily dressed children stood watching, and a small black and white dog nipped at the heels of one of the men. There were several stores, a post office, a blacksmith's shop with a glowing forge and many leather harnesses hanging on pegs. There was a fairly respectable looking tavern and near the outskirts of the village I could see the silver spire of a church and a large redstone building that may have been a school.

I could smell the delicious aroma of baking bread, mixed with the odors of rotten vegetables and cattle. An old woman in a black dress sat in front of a shop, making lace with nimble fingertips. She did not look down at her handiwork, but I could see that the piece in her lap was delicate and lovely. Lace made by the women of Lockwood Village was quite famous and London ladies of fashion paid a good price for it.

Although there were many people in town this afternoon, no one spoke to us. Indeed, they did not even look up, although I was sure that all of them observed us carefully and would discuss every last detail of our dress and appearance once we were gone. These people were taciturn, not at all friendly to strangers in their midst. Mr. Patterson had told me I would be quickly accepted after they found out I was my aunt's niece, but of course the villagers could not know that yet.

A boy named Billy Johnson came to drive us to Dower House. He had a large open wagon with one broad seat, and he began to pile the luggage in the back. Billy was twenty-three years old, strong, stocky and good natured. He wore a tight sleeveless leather jerkin that displayed his broad shoulders and muscular arms to good advantage, and his skin had been bronzed by the sun. He had an unruly mop of light brown hair and his eyes were the color of old pennies. He grinned at Nan and I knew that she had made her first conquest. Billy made his living doing any odd jobs that came along and by hiring himself out to the farmers when an extra hand was needed. He told us that he was saving for a cottage of his own where he could take his bride.

"You're married?" Nan asked, her mouth turning down in disappointment.

"Not yet, Ma'am."

"You have a girl?"

"Not a steady one. There's Betty Bransten—"

"Who is she?"

"A girl not half so pretty as you, Ma'am."

Nan gave him an encouraging smile and he helped us up to the seat. The dappled-gray horse trotted briskly down the street, kicking up a cloud of dust. Soon the village was behind us and we were driving on a tree-lined road that led through a thick woods. Billy talked pleasantly about himself and his ambitions and directed discreet questions towards Nan. She would not commit herself, but we were not a mile away from the village before it was firmly established that Billy would deliver all our groceries and supplies for us and be available any time we needed him.

The country was rich and green and thick with trees. I saw dark, shadowy pathways beneath the boughs, leading to cool isolated forest clearings. Golden sunlight sifted through the leaves, making a hazy, golden veil. We soon entered what appeared to be a private park, the rugged wilderness giving way to a more orderly arrangement. We passed through a gateway made of old stone columns, the rusty iron door held back, and the drive beyond it was lined with elm trees. We drove for a long time before I saw the house in the distance.

It could not properly be called a house. Castle, perhaps, would be a more suitable term. It was huge, sprawling over several acres of land, a vast pile of ugly stone adorned with turrets and wings and arches, brownish gray in color. There were hundreds of windows, and the sunlight glittered on the glass, throwing off silver reflections. It sat far back from the road, but even from the distance I could see that it was in a poor state of repair. Wooden platforms had been put up outside one wing, and men were climbing over them, working on the house.

"That's Phoenix Hall," Billy said. "And those men you see are doing repairs. Roderick Mellory brought them all in from Devon, would not give the work to the men of Lockwood."

"Do the workmen live at the house?" I asked.

"They put up shacks in back—far away from the house. They stay there, when they're not raising hell in Lockwood. There is over fifty of them. Loud, crude fellows who seem to think that the maids of Lockwood were created especially for their pleasure. There's been a lot of fights, even a knifing. The people blame Roderick Mellory for all of it, and rightly so."

"How long will the men remain at Phoenix Hall?" Nan asked.

"For another month, at least," Billy replied.

"Why did he bring them from Devon?" Nan inquired.

"For meanness," Billy said, "meanness of heart and of purse. He wouldn't pay the men of Lockwood decent wages, and they refused to do the work. So he imported these louts from Devon. They'll work for a pittance."

"The men of Lockwood must hate Roderick Mellory," I said.

"He ain't out to win their hearts, that's for sure," Billy said. "I think he relishes their hatred. He wants to be hated and feared. It gives him a sense of power."

"I should think he would be the one to have fear," I said, "with all that feeling against him."

"If he weren't his father's son, he might wake up someday with a knife in his stomach. But he is gentry, and he is Bradford Mellory's son. That fact protects him when nothing else would."

"They loved Bradford Mellory, didn't they?"

"If ever a man was more loved by the people I don't know who. He was like a saint."

"And his other children? How do the villagers feel about them?" I asked.

"Miss Laurel is exactly like her father. She does all she can for the people and would do more if her brother didn't interfere. She takes care of the sick and poor when she can, but her brother keeps her away from the people as much as possible. He doesn't want her to be contaminated by the peasants."

"And the boy, Paul? What about him?"

"No one sees much of Paul Mellory. He's lame, you know. He stays confined to the Hall and its grounds. I don't suppose he's been seen in the village for five years."

"What an unusual family," I remarked.

"You'd do best to keep away from them, Miss Todd," Billy said. "A young woman like you—" He clicked the reins, failing to complete his statement. "Some mighty strange things have been happening hereabouts. I'd hate to see you get involved in any of it."

He drove on silently and did not elucidate this remark. Nan let out a little cry as she saw a deer wandering across the road. It was a beautiful animal with a silky beige coat and silver-brown antlers. It paused to watch our progress with pensive brown eyes. Billy pointed out a salt lick to us and said that the Mellorys had a number of deer in the park, tame creatures who roamed at will over the green lawns and through the woods. He said I would see many of them near the Dower House and beside the stream.

"They don't come too near your place, though," he remarked. "In the past your aunt set up traps to keep them out of the garden. They used to trample her herbs and vegetables, and she waged war on them. She was a grand old woman."

"Did you know her well?"

"I used to make deliveries to the house," he said, "and once, when my ma was ill, your aunt came and watched over her and made the pain go 'way. You don't resemble her, Miss Todd."

"She was my mother's sister. I take after my father."

We rounded a bend in the road and I saw the Dower House for the first time. It sat beneath the shade of several large oaks and their large limbs cast soft purple shadows over the bleached gray stone. It was two stories with a green slate roof and a crumbly red chimney. The front door was painted green and there were green shutters at all the windows. It was a small house, compact and lovely, bearing its age with a faded grace. There were flower beds in front and gardens on both sides.

I could find no words to express my emotions. I was speechless at the beauty and serenity of the place. It was like something out of a dream. After so many years in a shabbily furnished boarding-house, I was to live in this home, and it belonged to me. I sat staring at it, seeing it all through the soft mist of tears. Billy unloaded our luggage and set it on the porch. A sleepy brown and yellow cat crawled up to watch the process. Nan lifted her canary cage high and shooed the cat away.

Mr. Patterson had given me the key to the door, and I opened it, directing Billy to move the bags into the front hall. I did not go inside at first. I wanted to wait a few moments until I had proper control of my emotions. I suppose this was the happiest event in my life and all by the grace of an eccentric old woman I had never known.

"You'll need some wood chopped," Billy said, finishing with the bags, "and I'll come round this afternoon to cut it for you."

"That would be nice," Nan told him.

"I'll bring some fresh eggs and butter and milk, and you can make a list of things you'll need in the way of provisions. Is there anything else I can do now?"

"I don't think so," I replied. I took a few coins out of my bag, preparing to pay him. Billy refused the money. He claimed meeting us was all the payment he needed, and although he used the plural form of pronoun his eyes were on Nan alone. She gave a little curtsy, standing on the porch to watch as he drove away.

"A fine lad," she remarked, smiling to herself.

"Indeed," I replied, calmer now.

"Shall we go into our new home, Miss Angel?"

I took her hand and we went inside. It was cool

and dark, and I threw back the shutters to let the sun come in. In a moment the rooms were flooded with silvery white light. Although it had been closed up for a while and had a faint odor of dust and dampness, the house was fragrant of home, of decades of wood fires and flowers, spices and herbs, of people who had lived here and left. There was the aroma of old wood that had been scrubbed and waxed for years.

Nan and I spent two happy hours exploring the place, going over each room and commenting on it and fingering all the things it held. I was pleased with the simplicity of everything. The walls were a faded gray, silvered with age, the floors golden brown hardwood that shone from years of beeswax rubbed into the grain. The furniture was simple too, hard, sturdy pieces of oak cut down to size, without the ornamental carving so prevalent in this Victorian age. The house was all bright and simple and comfortable, a place in which to live an uncomplicated, orderly life.

Upstairs there were two bedrooms, one large, one small. I chose the larger one for myself. It looked out over the gardens, and far away, over the tops of the trees, one could see the gables of Phoenix Hall. On the lower floor there was a study with oak desk and bookcase, a small parlor and dining room and a compact little kitchen with a blue and white tiled fireplace, a huge black stove and a zinc drain board. A huge black iron pot hung in the fireplace and black cooking utensils hung neatly on the walls. There was a tiny bedroom next to the kitchen and Nan decided she would prefer it to the extra room upstairs.

A door in the kitchen opened onto the stone steps that led to the cellar. It was very large, very cool down there, and so dark that we had to light a candle to see our way with. Unlike the rest of the house, it was cluttered and messy in the cellar. On the shelves were hundreds of jars of pickles and preserves and other foods, all neatly labeled, but strands of silky cobwebs stretched over them, and dust coated the tightly sealed jars. On the floor were stacks of jars, pots, boxes, old discarded tools, a broken spinning wheel, a litter of all the things there was not room for upstairs.

The cellar was as large as the lower floor of the house, and it had a musty, unpleasant odor I did not recognize. There was something I did not like about the place, something creepy and indefinable. I felt the cold dampness of the place and sensed something wrong, something I could not put a finger on. Nan stood on the bottom step, holding the candle. It flickered and spluttered, casting wild shadows over the walls.

"I don't like this place," she said.

"So you feel it, too?" I replied. "Something—wrong."

"Let's go up, Miss Angel. I feel a chill."

"What's that odor, Nan?"

"I don't know. I only know it's not right."

I felt something like fear, standing there on the earth floor, and I tried to laugh at myself, knowing it was foolish to feel this way. The cellar was messy, it smelled bad, but there was nothing wrong. Or was there? The place seemed so incongruous with the neat, bright rooms upstairs.

I stepped over to one wall and looked at the opaque brown jugs sitting beside some tiny wooden boxes that contained what looked like dried grasses and roots. I assumed they were some of my aunt's herbs, but the odor of them was acrid and bitter. Several small jars contained a cloudy green liquid and there were skull and crossbones scratched on the surface of the glass.

"Poison," I said. "All kinds of poison."

"Poison!" Nan cried.

"All kinds of it. I suppose my aunt made it."

"Whatever for?" Nan asked, shivering.

"Why—for insects, I suppose, or rodents. Perhaps she sold it to the farmers."

"Let's hurry, Miss Angel," Nan pleaded.

We went back upstairs into the sunny brightness of the kitchen. Nan closed the cellar door, and I was resolved to buy a lock and chain to put on it. There was no apparent reason for the distaste I felt for the cellar, and yet I felt it, strongly. Nan had felt it, too.

"Let's go out in back," I said. "I could use the fresh air."

The gardens in the back of the house were neat, the beds lined with gleaming white shells, a flagstone path leading from the back door to the gray stone well. An old oaken bucket dangled by its rope, and I dipped it into the water and pulled it up. I ladled out some of the water and tasted it. It was incredibly cold, deliciously fresh. There was a neat small smokehouse behind the garden, damp and cool inside, with hams and bacon and salted meat hanging from pegs. In the metal cooler there were blocks of cheese and butter wrapped in wet white cloths, even a dozen or so eggs, light brown and speckled.

"It seems that we are well provided for," Nan said.

"My aunt died so suddenly. All these things must have been here at the time of her death."

"Those hams look good. I will take one inside to cook."

"Isn't this smell heavenly?" I remarked.

Nan and I walked past the gardens and down a long slope to look at the deserted granite quarries Mr. Patterson had spoken about. They were an interlinking series of great cavities in the earth, all jagged and raw and ugly. They were deep and covered several acres with large, sharp rocks marking the walls and huge boulders littering the floors. If someone fell, it could mean instantaneous death. There had once been a wooden railing around the outer edges, but it had rotted away and collapsed in a heap of splintered slats. I kicked one of the slats with the tip of my shoe and sent it hurtling down into the quarry. It fell for a long time and then smashed on the rocks with a loud crash. Nan gripped my hand.

"We'll want to stay away from here," she said emphatically.

"It's a good thing there are no children about," I remarked.

We went back inside and began the long process of unpacking. It would take a long time for us to settle in properly. We found linen in the hall closet, fine sheets scented with verbena, and we made up the beds. I wiped dust off the surfaces of furniture, eager to begin a thorough spring cleaning tomorrow morning.

The sun was setting when Billy Johnson returned. He had a loaf of bread his mother had just baked, a pail of milk, some eggs and a small block of butter. Nan greeted him with enthusiasm and put him to work chopping wood for the fireplace. He came into the kitchen with a pile of small neat logs, which he put into the wood box beside the fireplace. I had just made a pot of coffee.

"Won't you sit down and have a cup of coffee with us?" I asked.

He smiled happily, pleased that he would be allowed to stay with us a little longer.

"This place already looks different," he remarked. He straddled a chair, his arms resting on the back, his chin resting on his arms. He was watching Nan as she laid the fire, his penny colored eyes full of sparkle. His great size made the sturdy chair seem small.

"How do you like your new home, Miss Todd?" he asked me.

"I think it is beautiful," I replied, smiling.

"It'll look nice after we clean up a bit," Nan agreed. "I made a list of things I'll need for tomorrow, and I want you to bring them first thing in the morning, Billy Johnson." Her voice was bossy, but Billy liked it. I thought him rather like a very large puppy.

"It is certainly quiet here," I remarked. "So peaceful. I feel as though I were hundreds of miles away from everyone."

"I'd be a little happier if we weren't quite so alone," Nan said. "It gives me a funny feeling not knowing there is someone nearby, near enough to hear a scream, for instance."

"Surely you're not frightened, Nan?" I said, laughing.

"Of course not," she snapped, though not convincingly. "I just don't like being so isolated."

Billy grinned, seeing an opportunity to tease her.

"You could scream all you wanted," he said, "and no one would hear you."

"Why should I scream?" she asked. "Surely there aren't prowlers about?"

"Some say the highwaymen have their hideout in this area. Lights have been seen in the deserted quarries and in the woods, usually soon after there has been a holdup. A farmer looking for a lost calf in the woods one night claims to have seen a figure in black walking near the quarries. He might have imagined it."

"Surely you're teasing, Billy," I said.

"No, Ma'am," he replied. "There's been lots of talk about the robbers' den being hereabouts. There's been search parties, but no one has ever found anything. But the lights have been seen, curious lights like hooded lanterns in the quarries and in the woods. Folks stay away from both places at night."

"My aunt was never bothered," I said.

"No one has been bothered. There have been no incidents, except for old Hatcher seeing the black figure, and Hatcher isn't a very reliable witness. He hits the bottle a bit too often."

Nan's face had grown a little pale, and Billy grinned when he noticed it. He was mischievous by nature and enjoyed frightening her. I could see the boyish devilment sparkling in his eyes.

"Of course there was a lunatic loose in these parts once," he continued. "He had a butcher knife he had stolen when he escaped from the Home. Belle James was coming through the woods one night after she had left her boy friend —she was a flighty thing, always doin' what she had no business doin'—and she met up with him. They found her next morning, a pitiful sight to see."

"And—did they catch him?" Nan asked.

"Not for a while. The men roamed all through
the woods with torchlights burning, and they
could hear insane laughter. It took them two days
and nights, but they finally rounded him up. Poor
man was curled up in a cave, babbling like a
child. The blood-stained butcher knife was beside
him."

"You hush now," Nan cried. "I don't want to
hear any more. It's all nonsense, anyway! Nothing
is going to hurt Miss Angel and me. Not while I'm
in possession of all my senses. Let me tell you
what I said to the highwayman when he held us
up last night—"

Nan began to babble about the holdup, and
Billy continued gazing at her with admiration. I
was glad when Billy finally left, for it was late
now and I was very tired. Nan told me that he had
asked her to go berry-picking with him at the end
of the week. She was undecided about going but,
holding her head to one side, she guessed that a
good berry cobbler would be nice. After a while
she went to her room and I undressed to go to
bed.

It was very dark outside, with only a few frosty
stars in a black sky. The limbs of the trees rustled
in the wind, and I could hear the boughs groaning, the leaves rattling. Crickets chirped, and I
heard a dog howling to the night from somewhere far off. I was far too excited and far too
happy, and I lay in bed in a state of semicon-
sciousness and watched the shadows creep across
the floor to the edge of the bed. Like Nan, I felt
the isolation of Dower House. It was strange not
to be able to hear all the noises of London that
had sometimes kept me awake when I was at the
boardinghouse. No carriages rumbling over the

cobbles, no horses' hooves, no nocturnal footsteps moving down the street. Here there was
only a serene silence that gradually lulled me to
sleep.

I awoke with a start, completely awake, every
sense alert. I had the acute sensation that something was wrong, and the strange, eerie feeling
that always comes when one is awakened in the
middle of the night. The room was very cold. The
window was open, and the chilly breeze blew the
curtains inward. They were billowing and rustling. Something had happened. In my sleep,
even, I had been aware of it, and it had torn away
the layers of unconsciousness and sent me hurtling into a state of tingling awareness. I sat up
now, trying to recall what had happened. There
was that sensation of aftermath, the air still full
of the reverberations of something that had just
taken place. The house was still and silent but for
the sound of the curtains flapping in the breeze.
My heart was pounding and my throat was dry.

I slipped into my robe, tying the belt with nervous fingers. I had just finished when I heard
someone moving downstairs. I stepped to the
door of my bedroom and opened it, listening. I
heard footsteps on the staircase. My hand flew to
my throat. It was paralyzed. I couldn't scream.
The steps came up, and I saw the flickering glow
of a candle.

Nan came into the hall. She was holding the
candlestick with a hand that was trembling visibly. The guttering orange light revealed a face
pale, with enormous eyes. Her white lace night
cap was askew on top of her head. She gave a
start when she saw me standing in the doorway.

"You heard it too?" she whispered hoarsely. "I was coming up to awaken you."

"What are you talking about, Nan?"

"The noise. There's someone in the cellar, Miss Angel."

"Nan—"

"I heard them. It sounded like someone moving something across the floor. And then there was a loud crash, like something had fallen. That must have awakened you."

"You—surely you imagined it." My voice trembled.

"No. I wasn't sleeping well after all those stories Billy told me. I kept imagining things. Then I heard the noises in the cellar. And they were not my imagination."

"Something woke me up, too," I whispered.

"The crash. It was enough to wake the dead."

We stood there in the hall for a moment, staring at each other with frightened faces. The candlelight cast wavering shadows on the wall. Nan was shaking with fright, and I was far from calm, but I tried to use my common sense. Hysteria would help neither of us.

"Are both the front and back doors locked?" I asked.

"Yes. I checked both of them before going to bed."

"Are you certain?"

"Of course."

"Then there can't be anyone in the cellar, Nan. No one could have gotten down there unless they came through the kitchen."

"But someone is down there!" she insisted.

"Nonsense," I said.

I was calmer now, at least outwardly. Inside I

was still trembling. I drew a deep breath and tried to control myself. It wasn't possible for anyone to be in the cellar if both the doors were locked. No one could possibly have broken into the house without Nan and me both hearing them, for the windows had all been securely fastened and an intruder would have had to have broken the glass.

"We'll go down and check the doors and all the windows," I said.

"Oh, Miss Angel—"

"Hush, Nan. Where is the courage you showed with the highwayman?"

"I could *see* him," she protested.

"Come on."

Although both of us moved slowly and as noiselessly as possible, our footsteps sounded loudly on the staircase. The silence of the house magnified every small noise we made and repeated it with soft echoes. Nan was calmer now as we went through each room, checking the windows. The house still had an air of strangeness about it for us, and I felt curiously as though we were the intruders.

We stood in the kitchen, every door and window checked. All of them were as we had left them. No one had tampered with any of them. We stood listening, hearing nothing but our own breathing. By now I was convinced that the noises in the cellar had all been Nan's imagination and that all that had awakened me had been her movements as she got out of bed. She was a little doubtful herself, looking at me with a frown on her face.

"I *did* hear something, Miss Angel."

"You're certain?"

"As certain as I am that we're standing here."

"Very well—we'll go down and check the cellar."

"Do—do we have to?"

"Neither of us will sleep unless we do," I replied.

The cellar door creaked as I opened it. The noise was loud and unpleasant. The cold, damp air came up, giving me a clammy feeling. Nan drew back a little as I stepped on the damp stone steps. The light of our candle wavered wildly in the sudden swoop of air, and for a moment I thought it would go out. I cupped my hand around it and proceeded on down the steps.

I was not brave, I was merely determined. I had had a bad fright, and I wanted to quell it. My whole body was rigid as I moved down the steps, but I forced myself forward. My common sense told me that there was no one in the cellar, my intelligence told me that it was very foolish to be afraid, but my emotions caused me to hold my breath with each step.

It was very dark, and the candle afforded little illumination, yet there was light enough to see that the cellar was deserted. No one stood behind the boxes and old trunks, no one crouched behind the old spinning wheel. There was dust and cobwebs and the acrid odor I had noticed earlier. There was a new odor, too, sharp and bitter and repellent. It had not been there this afternoon. I stood in the middle of the earthen floor, holding the candle high and watching the shadows playing on the walls. It was clammy and uncomfortable and sinister down here, and I had that same uneasy feeling I had had this afternoon, but no one else was in the cellar.

Nan stood on the steps, looking around at the

disorder, ready to fly back upstairs if anything moved. She was still frightened, and we examined the whole cellar in silence. I was curious about the new odor. I was certain I had not smelled it earlier. Nan smelled it, too.

"What is that smell?" she asked. "It wasn't here before."

"I—I don't know."

"It's nasty," Nan said.

"Are you sure it wasn't there this afternoon?" I asked.

I was certain of it myself, but I wanted Nan to confirm it. There was no reason for the smell to have materialized since we were down here in the afternoon. It gave me a queer, uneasy feeling, and for a moment I wondered if someone *could* have been in the cellar. I looked anxiously about in the dark corners, but they were empty. Then I saw the broken jar. It was in a dozen pieces on the floor beneath the shelf of poisons. There was a small pool of liquid, and the smell rose up from it.

"How—how did it fall?" Nan whispered.

"I don't know," I replied quietly.

"Someone was here! Someone knocked it off!"

There was a loud rustling at my feet. Something scurried over the floor. Nan screamed. I almost dropped the candle. The flame flickered furiously. I closed my eyes tightly, trying hard to keep from screaming myself. The large gray rat disappeared under a pile of sacking. Nan was beside me, gripping my arm. Then we both began to laugh hysterically. The laughter succeeded in releasing the tension.

"That's the answer," I said finally, weak with relief.

"The rat knocked the jar off the shelf. That's what we heard."

"Come, Nan," I said, leading her up the stairs.

The rodent provided a logical explanation for both the noise and the broken jar. It should have satisfied both of us. Nan was relieved, ready to laugh at herself and make light of the whole thing as we closed the cellar door. I was convinced that the cellar was empty and that the rat had knocked over the jar of poison, but I wished that I could dispel the feeling of uneasiness about the cellar. Something wasn't right. Something was there that shouldn't be there, an aura, an atmosphere that would continue to make me uncomfortable until I discovered what it was.

4

*T*he morning could not have been more beautiful. The air had a fresh and sparkling quality and the sky was pale blue. A bird singing in the tree beside my window had awakened me early, and I opened my eyes to the trilling music of his song. The nightmare quality of last night was gone. I could see now how foolish both Nan and I had been. Both of us had been tired and overstimulated and had let a broken jar upset us. How ridiculous. I smiled as I got out of bed, feeling that a glorious new day was in store for me.

There was so much to do, floors to sweep and scrub, furniture to dust and polish, windows to clean, drawers to rearrange. It would keep both of us busy all day, and there would be no time to dwell on the mystery of the cellar. Nan had awakened much earlier than I, and I could hear her singing a cockney ditty as I went downstairs. I could smell a heavenly aroma of food from the kitchen, and I went in to find sausages and golden yellow eggs and a plate of hot biscuits. Nan met me with an effusive smile. She looked fresh and pert in a dress of jade green cotton with a starched white apron tied about her waist.

"What a beautiful breakfast," I cried. "You'll spoil me, Nan."

"That's what I'm for," she replied.

I wondered what I would ever have done without her. I suppose it was a blessing for both of us. She would have a better life here in the country with me than she would ever have had in London, and if her encounter with Billy Johnson was any indication, it would not be a dull one.

After breakfast we set to work cleaning up the house. We were soon in a flurry of soapsuds, mops, polish, rags, wax and broom, and it was thrilling to see the floors sparkle with new golden highlights as we rubbed the wax in, to see the rich grain of the furniture gleam after we polished it. Nan took down all the curtains and washed them in a big pot in the back yard, stirring the soapy water with a large wooden spoon she had found. I began to wash the windows in the parlor. The glass had a fine blue sheen, and it sparkled with silver sunbursts as I cleaned away the dust and grime.

I was almost finished with the windows when I heard the carriage. It turned down the road and came up in front of the house. I wiped a strand of hair from my forehead and peered at the man who got out of the vehicle. He was very tall, with an athletic build and a graceful, fluid carriage of his body. His hair was light brown, and his features were extremely handsome—in a genteel way. He wore a pair of tight gray trousers and a plum colored frock coat. His boots were shiny black leather, and he wore a black silk tie flowing over the starched, ruffled white shirtfront.

He stuck the whip in its socket and whistled. A gorgeous silver gray dog leaped out of the carriage. It was a Borzoi and the most beautiful animal I had ever seen, elegant in every line.

Nan was in the kitchen, ironing the curtains, and I called her to go to the door. I had no idea who the visitor might be, but I did not want him to see me in a dirty cleaning dress. I hurried upstairs and changed, gave my hair a few rapid brush strokes and tried to compose myself. From my room I could hear the rich, husky voice of my visitor talking to Nan. I went downstairs, hoping my appearance was not too bad.

The gentleman rose when I stepped into the parlor. The first thing I noticed were his eyes. They were light gray, with tiny green specks, surrounded by thick, sooty lashes. They were gentle eyes, and the smile that played at the corners of his lips was a gentle smile.

"Miss Todd? I am Greg Ingram, a friend of your late aunt's."

"How do you do, Mr. Ingram."

"I thought I would return your property. It was given to me, for safe keeping, I suppose you'd say."

"My property?"

"Peter here," he said, pointing to the dog that was curled up in front of the fireplace, evidently at home, obviously contented. "He belonged to your aunt Lucille. I took him after she passed away. He is a fine animal."

"I should say so," I replied, kneeling to stroke his head. Peter took to me immediately, arching his neck so that I could scratch his ear and gazing at me with serene golden-brown eyes.

"I thank you for caring for him," I told my visitor. "You evidently did a fine job of it. He is in lovely condition."

"It was my pleasure, Peter was a good companion at the school. The boys loved him."

"You are a school teacher?"

"In a manner of speaking. Teacher, counselor, disciplinarian. We have twenty boys at the school —sons of the wealthier families in and around Lockwood—and I think of myself more as their friend than as their teacher."

"I am sure they must return the thought."

"Oh, for the most part, when we go for boating trips or picnics. A little less so when I try to drum Latin into their heads or have to use the rod."

"Do you use it often?" I inquired.

"Only when I have to," he replied matter-of-factly.

It was difficult for me to imagine Greg Ingram thrashing a boy. He seemed the epitome of gentility, a kind, intelligent man with an air of good breeding and background. Yet I could see how he would be firm. There was nothing soft about the man. He had strong, powerful hands, and his every movement was decisive. I judged him to be in his early thirties.

I asked Nan to bring us tea and we sat down. Greg Ingram sat on the chair in front of the window, his legs spread out in front of him and his palms gripping his knees. I noticed the sheen of his boots and the way he held his head a little to one side.

"I don't want to interrupt your work," he said. "I can see that you've had a very busy morning."

"Yes. We're trying to put the house in order."

"How do you like Dower House?" he asked.

"I think it's lovely."

"It has always been one of my favorite places in Lockwood. I came to visit your aunt quite often. Lucille was a Latin scholar, and she often helped me with a difficult passage in Virgil."

"She was? I didn't know my aunt read Latin. In fact, I know very little about her. She was a stranger to me."

"She was an enigmatic old woman," he said, his eyes turning inward as he reflected on the character of his deceased friend. "She was salty and even vulgar in ways, could brawl and curse with the best of them, yet her kindness and gentility at the bedside of a sick child or a dying man was something to behold. There was nothing she couldn't do if she put her mind to it. She discovered that she needed to know some Latin in her studies of herbs, so she purchased books and learned it. She was quite a reader, too."

He pointed to the books on the bookcase. There were dozens of them, bound in brown and gold leather, the color of their bindings contrasting nicely with the polished golden grain of the oak shelves.

Greg Ingram told me many stories about my aunt Lucille, and as he talked about her I began to feel that I knew her for the first time. She was eccentric, the black sheep of my mother's family, running off with a man far below her station and becoming a gardener's wife. Yet I felt her life, particularly the years spent at Dower House, must have been a rich and rewarding one, and I was sure that she had been happier than my mother ever was.

"What do you intend to do now, Miss Todd?" he asked.

"I don't know. I have no particular plans. I want to settle in and take long walks and get to know the countryside. I want to do some gardening, and I want to read all those books, and I want to meet the people who knew my aunt."

"Do you have a friend back in London?" he asked.

Although it was a very discreet question, I knew that he was referring to a male friend, a fiance. I blushed slightly, turning my head so that he would not see.

"No—" I replied. "I—there was no one."

"That's nice," Greg Ingram said.

I looked full into his eyes. They were smiling, and once again the strange beauty of them struck me. I blushed all the more, and I was relieved when he got up to leave. He paused to give Peter a final pat on the head and then asked me to attend services with him at the church. For a moment I hesitated, looking into his eyes, then I agreed to go with him the following Sunday. He said he would be by to pick me up, and we parted at the door. I watched him drive away, and I was still standing at the door when Nan came rushing into the hall.

"What a fine looking gentleman," she cried.

"Yes. He certainly is," I remarked.

"Such fine clothes, such manners. We'll have to fix up your lilac silk dress for Sunday."

"Nan! Were you listening?"

"No," she said evasively, "but I was in the kitchen ironing, and I couldn't help overhearing him ask you to go to church."

"What else did you hear?"

"Well—almost everything," she said slyly.

"So you like Greg Ingram?" I asked.

"Oh, yes. And you?"

"I—I think I like him, too," I replied.

Peter came up to me, holding his head up to be stroked. I rubbed my fingers over the silver gray fur as he watched me with adoring eyes. Nan looked at the animal a little dubiously at first, but I could tell that she was won over by his great beauty. Neither of us would be averse to having a watch dog after last night.

"Mr. Ingram is a fine spoken gentleman," Nan said. "And I know you made a good impression on him, Miss Angel. I could tell. His eyes lit up when you came into the parlor. Oh, I'm so excited—" She was already visualizing a romantic intrigue, no doubt, and I smiled at her foolishness. He was a fine gentleman, indeed, but I could see no reason why Greg Ingram should be interested in me. A man with his handsome looks and fine manners could doubtlessly have any girl he wanted, and I was sure he did not want me. Nevertheless, my heart felt lighter as I went back to my chores, and I spent a lot of time thinking about what I would wear on Sunday when he came to take me to church.

The rest of the week passed quickly for us. In three days we had Dower House sparkling. We put everything in order and there was not a surface that was not resplendent with polish or wax. I gathered up all my aunt's things and packed them away in a large trunk, reflecting sadly on the character of the woman who had left me this place.

The days were white and golden with sunlight,

the sky washed with gentle spring rain that caused wildflowers to crowd the hills. I worked in my aunt's gardens, pulling weeds, and fingering the rich brown soil. I studied several of the books on herbs in her small library, and it did not take me long to learn enough to care for the various plants. On my hands and knees, spading fork in hand, sunbonnet on head, I thought I could never know such peace and contentment.

We were so tired each night that we went to sleep quickly and gave no thought to the incident that had awakened us on our first night here. At any rate, we had Peter now. He slept in the hall, curled up on the thick blue rug that Nan had placed there for him. He quickly became as much a part of the household as Nan's canary who, perched in his cage in the kitchen, filled the lower floor with his singing. It seemed impossible that any other sort of life had ever existed. We spoke of Mrs. Clemmons and her dress shop as something distant, long ago in the past.

Billy Johnson became a part of the household, too, or so it seemed to me. He was at Dower House every day on some pretext or another, and while he helped with the chores and did many things that neither Nan nor I had the physical strength to do, he seemed to spend most of his time sitting in the kitchen chair admiring Nan and hindering her at her work. She scolded him with her sharp tongue, called him worthless and a pest, but this did not prevent Billy from coming back again and again. Sometimes they argued violently, for he had a quick temper and when he was angry the house seemed to shake with his rage. They both seemed to enjoy these verbal free-for-alls, each pushing the other to the extreme edge of fury and then standing back to witness the wrath. It was a sport Nan excelled at, and it kept boredom from setting in.

Billy brought us all the news from the village. He told us about the fight that had broken out on the square when some of the men working at Phoenix Hall came to town and tried to crash a dance the girls of Lockwood were giving. It had resulted in a brawl, and Billy had had a part in it, blacking several eyes and breaking one man's nose. Roderick Mellory had witnessed it all, sitting in his carriage and laughing. He had spurred his men on, Billy said irately, and had made no effort to help when some of the older men had tried to break the fight up. Billy also told us all the latest rumors about the highwaymen. Several professional men from London had come to Lockwood to ask questions and interview anyone who might possibly know anything about the holdups. They were sure that the bandits were stationed in or around Lockwood.

On Friday Nan and Billy went berry-picking. They came home with a huge bucket filled with juicy red dew berries, and Nan baked a cobbler. I noticed that her cheeks were rather flushed, and there was a secretive look about her eyes. She smiled coyly at Billy as he straddled his wooden chair. Billy's hair was mussed, and he had a sheepish look in his eyes. Nan was finding her own kind of happiness, and I was happy for her. I thought about Greg Ingram and wondered if I, too, would ever have that look of bliss.

I could tell that Greg Ingram was pleased when he saw me that Sunday. I was wearing an old dress of lilac colored silk, but Nan had adorned it with some fine black lace, and I thought it elegant and fashionable. My bonnet was purple velvet, with a broad black ribbon, and I carried a black string bag and a pair of black lace gloves. He stood for a moment just looking at me, his eyes reflecting his pleasure, and I was glad that I had taken such pains with my appearance. I told myself that this would be my first public appearance in Lockwood and that that was the reason I dressed with such care, but in my heart I knew that it was because I had wanted to see this look in his eyes.

"You look very nice, Miss Todd," he said.

"Thank you," I replied, highly complimented.

It was a long drive to the church, but it seemed all too short. He talked about his experiences at the schoolhouse and all the pranks that the boys pulled. I loved the sound of his voice, so rich and well modulated. It was like a kind of music. Ever so often he would turn to me with a smile. He was evidently enjoying himself, and I wondered if he had driven many young women to church in his smart carriage.

The countryside was lovely with the first touches of spring. Bright, hard little jade green buds were on some of the trees and the grass was turning a rich emerald shade, scattered with white and yellow wildflowers. We passed Phoenix Hall, and I was surprised to see that the workmen were busy at their repairs even on Sunday. I made no comment about it, but it struck me as strange. Roderick Mellory seemed to flaunt all the conventions.

Greg helped me out of the carriage in front of the church. We went into the church slowly, his arm linked in mine. I saw heads turn as we came in, but the people did not stare openly. Greg nodded to many of them. I kept my eyes downcast, slightly intimidated by all the strangers. For the most part they were simple people, strong, silent men with lined, weathered faces that showed years of hard labor, women with eyes that had seen many privations. They were soberly dressed in brown and black, and I felt rather out of place in my lilac silk.

The church was very plain, almost stark with whitewashed walls and a hardwood floor. The pews were of unfinished wood, rubbed smooth by hundreds of bodies, and there were no flowers about the plain wooden pulpit. The only touch of color was a small window of green and blue glass immediately behind the pulpit. It caused the whole front area to become illuminated with blue and green as the sun struck it. I sat quietly beside Greg, fingering the well worn hymnal and waiting for services to begin.

There was a slight stir in the back of the building. I heard something peculiar, as though wood was knocking on wood, but I didn't want to turn around. Then I saw the striking couple come down the aisle. The girl was very thin, dressed all in pink, her hair pale, almost silver. She held the arm of the tall, sensitive looking boy with brown hair. He was leaning heavily on her and on an elaborate cane for support. The cane knocked noisily as they proceeded on down the aisle and moved into the front pew.

I had no doubt that this was Laurel Mellory and her brother Paul. At least *they* respected the Lord's Day, I thought. I could not keep my eyes off them, and I continued to study them throughout the long, dull sermon delivered in a monotone by a somber, stern-faced preacher. There was no feeling of uplifting such as I had experienced every Sunday in my church in London. It was tedious and uninspiring until the congregation began to sing, and then I was moved almost to tears. These voices were not trained, nor were they particularly good, but they were rich with a sincerity that made them beautiful. Greg's voice was powerful, and he sang loudly, with conviction. My own voice seemed weak and timid.

After the services were over, we stood on the front steps and Greg introduced me to many of the people of Lockwood. They all seemed to be very fond of him, and he talked amiably about their interests, asking a woman about a sick child, speaking to a farmer about plowing. He was clearly quite popular, a polished, educated man who had established an immediate contact with the uncultivated villagers. I stood to one side as he carried on a conversation with the minister. I was a figure of interest to all the people, not only because I was Lucille's niece, but also because I had been on the coach when it was held up.

A group of men were talking loudly about the robbery. I heard them speaking of search parties and inquiries by the constable. The money had been intended as a government loan to the people of Lockwood. With it they would buy seed and farming tools and livestock. That it was coming on a passenger coach had supposedly been a secret, and there was much speculation as to how the highwaymen had known about this. Feeling was high, and for good reason. The men of Lockwood felt that one of their own had betrayed them by giving out the secret, or worse—one of them was the bandit.

I kept watching the door, hoping to see the Mellorys again.

I was soon rewarded. They came out in a few moments, the boy leaning on his sister. Laurel Mellory was pale, with shadows enveloping her dark blue eyes as though the lids had been stained with a light blue dye; her face had a sad, haunted look. She wasn't a pretty woman, but there was a delicate, fragile quality about her that was striking.

Paul Mellory had a sensitive face—marred only by the bitter curl of his mouth. His dark brown eyes, shadowy with thought, were clearly not the eyes of a happy man. He was handsome, with the broad shoulders and straight back of a soldier. It must be a terrible thing for one so young and so full of life to have to walk with a cane, supported by his sister, I thought. Yet, he carried himself with pride, even arrogance, and I wondered if he resembled his older brother. He turned his head sharply and caught me looking at him. For a moment our eyes met and held, and then he looked away, the curl of his lips even more pronounced.

What lost, miserable people, I thought, living in the luxurious vastness of the great house and yet each trapped in a small world of private torment. Laurel Mellory had been a failure in London. She was an old maid already, I thought, tall, thin, doing good works, lost to the world of romance. How many dreams must she have given up, how many bright plans must have vanished when she came back to the isolated mansion to live with a dying mother and two brothers. Paul Mellory was even more tragic. He could never live a man's life. His world must always be a narrow one. Books and music could never take the place of all the things that could never be his.

A large black carriage drove up and a servant got out to help them inside. As the carriage drove away I could see Laurel's pale, silvery blonde head against the cushion, and I could see Paul Mellory's eyes. He was staring at me with something like hatred, and I felt very weak inside. He must think that I was looking at him because of his leg. He must think that I was rude. If only I could have spoken to him.

The graveyard where my aunt was buried was in back of the church. Greg took me there, his fingers wrapped tightly about my elbow as we walked around the building. A high rock fence enclosed the yard, and a huge, ancient oak tree with spreading limbs grew in one corner. The limbs spread over most of the yard, making it dark and shadowy. Tall grass grew between the graves, and the markers for the most part were very old, cracked and yellowed with age. It was damp and chilly, and I stood close beside Greg as he pointed out the grave of my aunt.

"I wish I had known her well," I said.

"She would have liked you," Greg replied.

"Do you think so?"

"How could she have helped it? You are everything that a young woman should be."

"Why do you say that?"

"I think I am a qualified judge."

I looked into his eyes, wondering what he meant. I was not sure how I should take his remarks.

"You were a success with the villagers," he continued. "They do not show approval openly, but it's there if you know where to look. I could tell how pleased they were with you."

"I felt out of place," I said.

"You will, for a while. And then you will feel that you belong. It is a wonderful feeling."

"Do you belong, Greg?" I asked.

"To Lockwood? I suppose I do. I've been accepted. I have a role to fill, and I have a place, but no, I don't really belong here. I belong somewhere else."

I thought his voice had a curious tone.

"Where do you belong?" I asked.

He smiled, and it was a strange smile. "I wish I knew," he said. "Someday, perhaps, I'll find out . . ."

We left the graveyard and Greg took me to the schoolhouse to show me where he worked. It was closed up and locked for the weekend, all the boys sent home, but Greg had a key to the main door. He took me down a long hall and into the main classroom. I had an eerie feeling as I stood there looking at the twenty small wooden desks, each with its own ink pot. I recalled my own school days, and I thought there was something sad about this room. It smelled of chalk dust and ink, and it seemed to be still warm with the heat of young bodies. There was a bookcase crammed with old text books and stacks of paper, and a wooden podium faced the desks. The blackboard had Latin names written on it in large blocked letters.

"Here is where I try to pound knowledge into young skulls," Greg said, picking up the long wooden pointer and touching the blackboard with its tip. "Pretty impressive, aren't I?"

"Do you like teaching?" I inquired.

"It will do until—until something better comes along," he replied, smiling. "I like the boys. I enjoy working with them. They're healthy young animals and must be treated as such. I enjoy taking them on swimming jaunts and teaching them cricket. I get along nicely with them most of the time."

"But you're not happy?"

"Not happy? Not unhappy. Maybe I want bigger things. Lockwood is the world to those people you saw at the church. It isn't the world to me." He smiled again, shaking his head at me. "But I don't intend to bore you with the long list of my ambitions. I'll save that for some more appropriate time."

On the ride back to Dower House, he talked lightly and pleasantly as though to make up for the moment of seriousness at the schoolhouse. He had given me a moment of insight into his character, and I saw many things about Greg Ingram that I had not seen before. He was restless, and while contented to make the best of things for the time being, he was not satisfied with his lot as a country school teacher. He was certainly qualified for something much better, and I wondered how he had come to this unlikely place. Perhaps there was a story behind it that I would learn after I got to know him better.

We passed Phoenix Hall. Through the network of green leaves half-concealing it from the road, it looked like a child's toy left on the lawn, so small was it from this distance. The sunlight struck the old brown gables and turrets with yellow lights. Men were still working on the wooden platform, handing long pieces of lumber back and forth, and a stone mason was repairing brick work at one end. Although he had not commented on it before, Greg frowned now, creasing his brows deeply.

"Someday Rod will go too far," he commented, more to himself than to me.

"You know Roderick Mellory?" I asked.

He nodded. "I go to Phoenix Hall quite often. Paul is my friend, and we study together some. We both have an interest in English history, and we both love music. He is quite an accomplished pianist. You saw him at church? What a tragedy."

"He seemed bitter."

"Wouldn't that be natural? He's moody, sometimes sullen, but that is only a front. In reality he's extremely sensitive, introspective. I am very fond of him."

"Is he like his brother?"

"Like Rod? Not at all. Roderick Mellory is the devil incarnate," he said, his voice harsh. "He has one ambition, to make Phoenix Hall what it was in the past—one of the greatest estates in the country—and he will stop at nothing to see that that ambition is fulfilled."

"He wants Dower House back," I told Greg.

"He has wanted it for a long time. You know about the law suit?"

"Yes."

"That didn't work. When your uncle died he offered your aunt much money if she would sell the place back to him. She laughed at him. It was her home, and Roderick Mellory had no rights to it."

"Why does he want it so badly?"

"I suppose he hates the thought of strangers living on the estate, people he has no control over. It affects his sense of power. Everyone must bow to the authority of Roderick Mellory, and when he cannot make someone bow to this authority, it infuriates him. Lucille would not bow. Her obstinacy made him all the more determined. Has he approached you about selling?"

"Only through my lawyer," I said.

"He will, rest assured of that."

"I am afraid Roderick Mellory will find someone else who will not bow," I replied.

We drove the rest of the way to Dower House in silence. Greg left me at the door, and I stood there a long time, thinking of all he had said. Peter came up to keep me company, and I stroked his head. I had learned a lot today. My curiosity about the Mellorys was all the more intense after seeing the boy and girl at church. I wondered if Roderick Mellory would really come to see me about selling the house. I did not know, but I knew that the Master of Phoenix Hall would be mistaken if he thought he could use his evil influence over me.

I rested at the spring, sitting on the bank beneath the heavy shade of the trees whose limbs met over the water, making a dark green canopy, alive with birds. The leaves rustled, and a few rays of sunlight filtered through to sparkle on the flowing water. I sat still and it was not long before a fawn came to drink. He moved silently, and he paused at the edge of the water to look around with brown velvet eyes. I saw his delicate limbs and his spotted fur. I moved, and he looked up at me, poised for flight, then continued to drink.

My basket was half full of flowers as I penetrated deeper into the woods. It was dark and damp and full of the wonderful aromas of spring. I had no destination in mind, at least not consciously, yet when I got to the clearing at the edge of the woods and stared at Phoenix Hall, it seemed that I had intended to come here all along. I was directly behind the clumsily constructed shacks of the workmen, a dozen or so wooden huts thrown up any which way. Piles of lumber and stacks of brick littered the area, and there were bags of mortar, coils of rope, kegs of nails. I saw trash and debris and thought the place was rather like a small slum area in back of the mansion. I knew from Billy that the repairs would be completed soon and that the men would all go back to Devon soon after the first of May.

I turned to leave. I did not want anyone to think that I was spying. I was rather nervous and apprehensive at being so near the place. Phoenix Hall held nothing good for me, and I did not want to be found near it. I did not hear the footsteps behind me, and I let out a little cry as the hand gripped my arm.

"Hey, fellows! Look what I've found."

The man was large and burly with a hard, leathery face and ugly gray eyes that danced with malice. His thick lips were curled into a leer. He wore a pair of dusty black boots, tight brown pants and a tan shirt with the sleeves rolled up over his muscular arms. The fingers gripped my arm tightly. I tried to pull away and he jerked me closer to him. Two more men came around the corner of one of the shacks. They were dressed exactly like the first and had the same blunt peasant features.

"Let go of me," I said, trying to keep calm.

"Now, little Lady—keep still."

"What have you got there?" one of the men asked, grinning.

"Little local lass. She's probably heard how nice we were and come to see for herself. Yeah—that must be it."

"Pretty little thing."

"Brung us some flowers, too."

"Don't squirm so, Lassie," the man holding me said.

I held my breath. I must keep calm. I tried to summon all my mental resources to prevent hysteria from overcoming me. The other two men crowded around me. I could see their eyes gleaming with malice, and I could smell their breath. They were crude, common, ugly men, with no morals. I thought of all the tales Billy had told us about them, and I shuddered. There was nothing I could do. If I screamed I would bring more of them. I could not break away. I had to use my intelligence. I had to outthink them. My voice trembled as I spoke.

"Let—let go of me," I said. "You don't seem to know who I am. I—I'm the minister's daughter. I came to—to see Miss Laurel, and I will tell Mr. Mellory if you don't release me—now."

"Listen to her."

"She's lying. The minister doesn't have a daughter."

"No young ladies call on that Miss Laurel. Ain't one been to see her since we've been working here."

"Naw—the girls in town told 'er about us. She came to have some fun, and your ugly face scared her, Burt."

The man called Burt held my arm tightly. I tried to jerk away. He pulled me around and pinioned me against his chest, one arm around my waist, the other about my shoulders. He was breathing heavily.

"What we goin' to do with her?"

"I found her. You all go on back—"

"That ain't no way to be now, Burt. We'll take her to the shack."

"Yeah—"

I placed my hands against the man Burt's chest. I drew in a deep breath and then shoved with all my might. He stumbled backwards, and I was free for a moment. I tried to run. One of the men caught my skirt. I jerked it free, and I could hear the material ripping. I ran toward the clearing, but I got only a few steps when a hand grabbed my arm and another seized my hair. My bonnet had fallen off. The basket of flowers flew into the air. I could see the flowers flying, and then they were crushed beneath heavy boots as the men circled about me. I fought wildly, blindly, striking out like a person possessed of a demon. I caught a hand between my teeth and bit down hard until I could taste the blood. I raked my fingernails across a cheek, and I saw four red streaks where the flesh was torn. My head swam. My heart pounded. I was thrown onto the ground. The breath was knocked out of me. Through heavy lids I saw the men coming toward me.

And then I heard the scream. It sounded like the cry of a wounded animal, shrill, loud, pierced with agony. I saw the whip curling around the man's face, and when the black coils vanished there was blood dripping. I heard the loud slashing explosion as the whip flew through the air again, the sharp crack as it made contact with flesh. There was another scream. And another. I heard footsteps running away and curses shouted by a new voice. Then there was silence.

I tried to get up. My head was going round and round in circles. I felt a hand on my wrist, pulling me to my feet. I saw dark black eyes, burning with anger, and I had an impression of the face. My eyes were not focusing, and my head seemed to go round faster and faster. I felt my feet firmly on the ground and I tried to say something. Then everything began to swim and I fell forward. I felt the strong arms catch me up, holding me tightly, and then the black wings in my head fluttered, closing in, and I knew nothing.

I was first aware of the smell, sharp but not unpleasant, tantalizing my nostrils. The layers of black lifted slowly, turned gray, and then my eyelids fluttered and I seemed to see everything through a hazy fog. There was a dull ache at the back of my head, and my arms hurt where the fingers had gripped them so tightly. The room I was in was strange and I blinked my eyes, trying to get rid of the fog. My whole body felt heavy and the dull pain grew worse as I tried to sit up.

The room was dimly lighted, the heavy rose curtains drawn to, the sunlight coming through weakly. I was on a small sofa of rose velvet and there were several cushions under my head. I saw the walls papered with embossed gray material, and the rich old carpet of some crimson colored plush that had begun to fade. The furnishings were elegant and very old, candles in ornate old gold candelabra, chests of dark brown wood, highly varnished, a fading tapestry of peacock blue and green hanging on one wall, depicting some medieval scene. I tried to sit up but the pain was fierce. I fell back with a little groan and blackness enveloped me again.

It was much later when I awoke for the second time. The light was dimmer, darkly gold, indicating late afternoon. Some of the pain was gone, and the fog had vanished. There was a box of smelling salts on the table beside the sofa, and a cut glass decanter of brandy with two glasses on a heavy silver tray. The man was standing at the window. He had his back to me, and I saw his powerful shoulders encased in expensive black broadcloth. He was very tall, very straight, with long, well turned legs and thin hips molded in the same black broadcloth as his jacket. One large brown hand held the draperies back and the other was curled around the handle of the whip. The long black lash coiled on the crimson carpet like a serpent.

I sat up with a slight groan, supporting the side of my head with one palm, and the man turned around. We stared at each other for a moment, our eyes locked. I felt a shiver of fear rush through me as he carefully rolled the whip up, his eyes never leaving mine. He laid the whip on a side table and smiled, the corners of his lips turning up ever so slightly.

"Are you feeling better?" he asked.

"I—I think so."

"I don't think you were really hurt. You've had a hard knock on the back of your head—nothing more serious. No, don't try and get up just yet. Rest there for a while."

"Where am I?"

"You're in the parlor of Phoenix Hall."

"And you are—"

"Roderick Mellory, at your service."

He made a little mock bow, his dark black eyes burning with malice. That strange smile still hovered on his lips. He seemed to be enjoying my predicament. I still felt very weak. I rested on the cushions and closed my eyes for a moment. When I opened them the Master of Phoenix Hall was still staring at me. I felt uneasy. I wished those eyes would stop burning so fiercely as they examined me. Roderick Mellory came over to the table and poured a glass of brandy.

"Take this, Miss Todd," he said.

"You know my name?"

"I know everything there is to know about you, Miss Todd."

"What do you mean?"

"Exactly what I said. I know everything about everyone who lives on my estate. That includes you."

"Dower House is mine. It isn't part of Phoenix Hall."

"To your way of thinking, no."

"And to your way of thinking?"

"We won't go into that now, Miss Todd. Your lawyer told me that you had no intentions of selling it to me. So legally it is yours. We will let it rest at that for the present." His thick lips curled into the malicious smile. "We have other things to discuss, it would seem. Drink your brandy, Miss Todd."

I sipped the brandy. The fumes were strong and the liquid burned my throat. I could feel the warmth stealing through my body, and the strength began to come back. I drank the brandy slowly, while Roderick Mellory moved restlessly about the room, touching objects, moving things, looking out of place in this elegantly appointed room. I took this opportunity to study the man.

Raven black hair covered his head in unruly waves, so black that it had a dark blue sheen to it. It grew in narrow sideburns down his thin, tanned cheeks, and it curled in soft tendrils about the nape of his neck. The eyes were actually dark brown, so dark I had thought them black. The hooded lids were heavy, and the brows rose in winged arches, giving a truly demonical cast to his face. His nose had a hump at the bridge, as though it had been broken at some time. This was strangely attractive, I thought, unable to deny the powerful magnetism of the man. He had an aura of brutal strength, of arrogance, the air of a man who had always had his way and will see to it that he always has.

Roderick Mellory frightened me. I was afraid of him, as one would be afraid of a caged panther, and yet I had to admit that he was the most fascinating man I had ever seen.

"I am extremely sorry this—this incident took place, Miss Todd. I can assure you that the men have already been discharged and are already off the premises. They—uh—mistook you for another kind of woman."

"So it would seem," I replied.

"Your dress is badly torn. I will see to it that you have a new one immediately."

"You needn't bother, Mr. Mellory."

"Oh, but I shall," he replied, making the mock bow again. "I must do all I can to make up for this —unpleasantness. I do not want my new neighbor to have bitter feelings about Phoenix Hall."

I said nothing. I could feel my cheeks flushing, and my anger began to rise. I hoped that I could control it. Roderick Mellory already had me at a disadvantage, and I did not want to make it worse. He perched on an ivory upholstered chair and spread his legs out, then he leaned forward, lowering his voice to a casual, conversational tone I found exasperating.

"You look enchanting when your cheeks glow like that," he said. "In fact, I find you a very enchanting young woman, not at all what I expected when I heard that Lucille Dawson's niece had inherited Dower House."

"What did you expect, Mr. Mellory?" I asked tartly.

"A dried-up old maid, I'm afraid. Someone prim, prissy, given to charitable organizations and knitting."

"I'm sorry you're disappointed," I snapped.

"Oh, disappointment is hardly the case."

"Are you paying me a compliment?"

"A perceptive young woman would know that instinctively."

"Perhaps I'm not perceptive. And compliments will do you no good, Mr. Mellory. I have no intentions of letting you have Dower House. It belongs to me. You cannot charm me into changing my mind."

"Was I trying to charm you? Dear me, I didn't realize that." His tone was mocking. He grinned. "Your eyes are flashing, Miss Todd. You must not excite yourself. I would think you'd had enough excitement already for one day."

"Those awful men—" I began.

"One can hardly blame them."

"What do you mean?"

"You were there—a pretty young woman—on my property, trying to see what you could see—"

"I was here by accident," I protested.

"Accident? Surely one doesn't arrive at Phoenix Hall by accident, Miss Todd."

"I—I was gathering flowers in the woods. These woods are unfamiliar to me and I lost my way. I —I just found myself behind those shacks. I had no intentions of being here—to see anything." Even to my own ears this sounded unconvincing. Roderick Mellory only smiled.

"You lost your way?"

"Surely you don't think I would have come deliberately, not after all the terrible things I've heard about you." I hoped this barb would hit home. Instead of causing him concern, it seemed to delight him.

"You've heard terrible things about me?"

"Many terrible things."

"You believe all you hear, Miss Todd?"

"Not everything."

"If it's about me, you should believe it. I am quite bad. Anyone will tell you that."

"You sound proud of your reputation," I said.

"Proud? No, not proud of the gossip of a bunch

of yokels who have no understanding of a man with purpose. Not proud of stories that paint me as Satan. Proud that I am what I am, something those people can never hope to sympathize with. If they called me a saint instead of a devil, I would worry. My father was a saint. My father went bankrupt. I had to work like the devil they say I am in order to make up the losses. Phoenix Hall is in the clear now, because of the devil in me."

I was silent. I could think of no quick retort, and I had sensed a quality in the man that I could almost admire. I had worked to repay the debts my father had left when he died, and I could understand this about Roderick Mellory. I could almost see, for a moment, the purpose he spoke about, and I could almost sympathize with him in it, but I did not want him to know this. He would despise my sympathy more than anything else.

Roderick Mellory poured himself a glass of brandy and drank it with three quick gulps, jerking his head back as though it were distasteful. He stood in front of the sofa, his fists planted on his thighs, looking down at me as though I were an object needing close study. There was a frown on his face, the brows arching like black wings, the lips turning up at one corner wryly.

"You present quite a problem, Miss Todd," he said finally.

"Really?"

"Indeed you do. Quite a problem."

"How is that?" I asked.

"A young woman of your age and background, living alone at Dower House. I don't like it. I'm not sure that it's safe. If anything were to happen to you, I would feel responsible."

He spoke slowly, and each word struck me with terror. Was Roderick Mellory threatening me? He wanted Dower House desperately, and he knew that he could not buy it. He knew after talking with me that he could not talk me into selling it. His money and his persuasion would be to no avail. He was a man who would stop at nothing in order to get his way. Although I could not be certain that his words contained the threat, the menace of the man was evident as he stood over me. Threatening a defenseless woman would not be beyond him. He would find satisfaction in seeing me cringe.

I was not going to give him that satisfaction. I got to my feet, swaying just a little as a wave of dizziness swept over me. He took my arm to support me. I pulled it away.

"You needn't worry," I said. "I am quite capable of taking care of myself."

"Yes. We had a splendid example of that this morning."

"I must go now. My maid will be frantic."

"By all means. I'll summon a carriage."

"You needn't do that. I can walk back to Dower House."

He pulled a bell cord. He laughed softly to himself. "You are a proud young woman, Miss Todd. I find that admirable, but you cannot walk home at this hour and in your condition. It's almost dark and you are still weak." A servant came into the room and he ordered the carriage to be brought around. He led me down a long hall and as we waited for the carriage he took a huge black satin cloak and wrapped it around my shoulders, saying the driver could return it. He handed me my bonnet and empty flower basket and put me into the carriage. As it drove away I could hear him laughing. I looked back at Phoenix Hall and saw his dark form on the front steps, doubled up with amusement.

Nan had been frantic, as I had anticipated. If I had not come home when I did she was going to have Billy Johnson organize a search party. I told her simply that I had had a small accident and had been taken to Phoenix Hall. I did not mention the workmen or Roderick Mellory's timely rescue, feeling it would be wiser for all concerned if the details were not broadcast over the countryside. Nan plied me with all sorts of questions when she saw my torn dress and the bruises on my arm, but I was evasive. She asked me about Phoenix Hall and its Master. I merely said that I had met Roderick Mellory and that I had not taken to him at all.

Three days later there was a knock at the door and the same manservant who had driven me home that night handed me a large flat box. I was startled. The servant left without saying a word. I took the box into the parlor, extremely curious, but not nearly as much as Nan. While I opened the box and removed layer after layer of tissue paper she danced about the room in a state of intense excitement.

Roderick Mellory had promised to send me a new dress and he was good for his word. I wondered how he had obtained the dress so quickly, for it obviously didn't come from anyplace around here. I took it out carefully, and Nan gave a little cry of pleasure. I looked at the dress, my own reactions quite different. It was a deliberate insult, or else I was mistaken. Perhaps it was a bribe. I could never wear such a dress, not a woman of my station and background, and Roderick Mellory must have delighted in that knowledge when he picked it out.

It was pale white satin with an overlay of exquisite gold lace. The bodice was sewn with tiny seed pearls and scallop after scallop of thin gold lace adorned the skirt. The dress must have cost a small fortune. I had seen such gowns in the theater, and I knew that women of the Court must have worn such creations at State affairs. The dress was suitable for an actress, or for Royalty, but it was certainly not suitable for a former seamstress who now lived in the country.

There was a tiny white card, the handwriting in firm hard strokes of black ink. "A lovely gown for a lovely young lady. I hope to see you wear it soon. R. M." It was an insult, a deliberate blow at the pride I had displayed to him. I tore the card into small pieces.

"Such a gown!" Nan cried. "Whoever is it from—"

"Hush, Nan," I said sharply.

"You have a secret admirer. Someone very wealthy—" her eyes grew wide as she realized who must have sent the dress. "Mr. Mellory! He's the one who sent it. Oh, Miss Angel—"

"I must send the dress back," I said.

"Miss Angel, you can't do that. Such a lovely thing—"

I realized that she was right. I could not send the dress back to Roderick Mellory. That would give him too much satisfaction. He would be all too delighted to know that he had hit his mark. I would not let him know that. I began to lay the dress back in the box, folding the lace carefully and spreading the tissue paper over it. Roderick Mellory would never know my reactions to the dress. Quite simply, I would do nothing. I would not send the dress back, nor would I send a card to thank him. Silence was the only weapon I had against the man.

The next night Nan and I sat up very late in the parlor. Tomorrow was May Day, and both of us were going to the May Fete. Greg had informed me that he was going to have to take all the boys from school to the affair, and I would be an additional chaperone. Nan was going with Billy Johnson, and both of us were sewing on the dresses we would wear for the occasion.

One lamp burned on the low parlor table, and our chairs were drawn up on either side of it. We sat in a pool of warm yellow light, all our sewing things in our laps. It was a comfortable feeling to be surrounded by the silence and serenity of the house. The walls of the parlor were covered with old ivory paper with tendrils of dark green leaves, and the carpet was dark green, faded. The furniture was golden oak, simple and serviceable, and the lamp light shone dimly on the rows of books with their brown and gold leather bindings, I felt at ease, relaxed, having put aside my feelings about Roderick Mellory and now only looking forward to the pleasures of tomorrow and Greg Ingram's company.

Peter lay at my feet, curled up and drowsy, his sleek silver gray head resting on his front paws. Nan's canary sat on his perch, silently pecking at his seed. Nan was sewing bright pink ruffles on the white and green striped dress she would wear to dazzle Billy Johnson and, no doubt, all the other local lads. It was very late and I was sleepy.

I wanted to finish putting the stitches in my dress, however, and I sang a little song under my breath in order to keep awake.

Peter leaped up with a start, bristling. Nan dropped the ruffles, her mouth opening in surprise. For a moment we said nothing, both of us so startled by the dog's sudden action. Then we heard something outside the window, something moving. It sounded as though someone was in the garden directly in front of the parlor window. I turned off the lamp. I heard Nan give a little gasp as darkness engulfed the room.

"What—what is it, Miss Angel?" she whispered hoarsely.

"I don't know, Nan. If anyone is there, I don't want them looking in on us. Do—do you hear footsteps in the garden? Perhaps Peter had a bad dream—" I paused, listening. There was movement outside. I could not be sure what it was. Perhaps a cat, perhaps the wind blowing one of the tree limbs against the side of the house.

I stepped across the dark room to the window, pushing back the curtain and peering outside. It was a beautiful night, the moon riding on a bank of dark black clouds. It went behind the clouds temporarily, and the garden became a patchwork of velvety black shadows, relieved by tiny pools of silver. The shadows moved, but it was windy and the tree limbs groaned and waved, throwing dark arms of shadow over the garden. I was not greatly alarmed. There could easily be a logical explanation for the noise, and Peter could have been dreaming.

"Is anyone out there?" Nan whispered.

"I don't think so."

"But that noise."

"It must have been the wind, Nan."

"Oh."

Peter threw his head back and began to howl. Nan clutched her hands together dramatically. I squinted my eyes, peering out at the maze of shadows, seeing the flagstone path shining in silver glow, surrounded by the dark tree trunks, all in shadow. I saw the dark form of the wheelbarrow I had left in the garden and beside it the lumpy half full bag of manure Billy had brought me to fertilize the flower beds with.

Then I saw the dark form standing beside the oak tree. It was unmistakably human. I felt a cold chill creep over my body. Nan came up behind me, and she, too, peered out over my shoulder. We watched the man standing there, half leaning against the trunk of the tree. We could see that he was not very tall and had the stocky build of many of the local men. He held a large, flat object in his hand, but it was so dark that we could not tell what it was.

"Miss Angel—"

"Keep still, Nan. The doors and windows are all locked. He can't get in."

"What is he doing out there?"

"We'll soon find out."

He moved away from the tree. There was a loud whirring noise of something flying through the air. I pulled Nan away from the window just as it shattered with a splintering explosion of sound. Pieces of glass fell to the floor and something large rolled across the carpet. We heard noisy footsteps as the man ran away. Nan was near hysterics and I gripped her hand tightly. The sound of footsteps died away. It was silent but for Peter's whimpering. He pawed at my feet.

I turned on the lamp. There was a large rock in the middle of the floor, a piece of paper tied to it clumsily with some string. I picked up the rock and opened the note with trembling fingers. It was scrawled in large, half-formed letters, as though written by a child or someone who was not accustomed to pencil and paper. The message, however, was clear: LEAVE DOWER HOUSE AT ONCE. LEAVE BEFORE IT'S TOO LATE. I gave the note to Nan, and she drew in her breath, staring at me with large, frightened eyes.

"It's a prank, Nan," I said, "merely a silly prank."

"But—who sent it?"

I knew very well who had sent it. Roderick Mellory had tried to buy Dower House, and he had failed. He had talked with me, and he had seen that he could not persuade me to sell. He had failed there, too. I remembered the words that seemed to have contained a half-veiled threat when he mentioned my being alone at Dower House. Now I knew that the threat had been real. He could not buy Dower House and he could not persuade me to give it up, so now he was going to try and frighten me away. I smiled bitterly, my cheeks flushed with anger. Dower House belonged to me. It was mine and I loved it. Roderick Mellory was not going to frighten me into leaving it. He would fail in that as well. I was as stubborn as he was, and I did not frighten easily.

6

*T*he air rang with shouts of laughter and all the bright noise and confusion of a whole countryside at holiday. This was the one day when all chores were forgotten, when frets and worries were put aside. The green lawns on the outskirts of Lockwood were crowded with people of all ages, all of them intent on having a lighthearted, lusty time. Inhibitions were lost, and a permissive attitude guided everyone. Although not nearly so debauched as in the old days, these celebrations derived from the ancient Celtic Priapean ceremonies and the gaily adorned Maypoles still carried that significance. Maids with rosy cheeks were pursued by lads with sun-browned faces, while indulged parents looked on with good-natured smiles.

"They'll all be stone sober and taciturn again tomorrow," Greg said as we walked down the slope towards the river, "but today anything goes in Lockwood."

"It seems so contradictory," I remarked.

"They must let loose once in a while," he replied. "May Day gives everyone a chance to release pent up energies once a year. It gets very robust later on, particularly after the wine takes effect. You'll see fights and brawls; they're as much a part of May Day as the wrestling matches among the boys and girls, and everyone enjoys them."

He grinned. "Are you shocked, Angela?"

"Not particularly," I said.

"Queen Victoria wouldn't approve, but these Cornwall folks have a way of life all their own. Nothing straitlaced on May Day."

"So it would seem," I retorted.

There was a crowd of people down by the river, many of the men with goat skins swollen with wine. Accompanied by gales of laughter, they tipped their heads back and squirted the wine into their open mouths. Women in bright skirts and shawls watched over the children who eagerly waited to ride in the canoes that bobbed on the surface of the water. There was a group of young boys, all dressed identically in brown pants and little brown jackets, large black silk bows tied at their necks. They were accompanied by a sober-faced, middle-aged man who looked about disapprovingly. This was Greg's associate at the school, Mr. Stephenson, and he seemed to be having a difficult time restraining the boys.

"I must take them for a canoe ride," Greg said. "I promised. Will you come along?"

I shook my head. "You go on, Greg. I'll wander around and amuse myself. You'll find me near the carousel."

"You're sure you don't mind?"

"Of course not."

I watched as Greg helped herd the boys into three canoes. They were bubbling with excitement and making so much racket that Mr. Stephenson's voice, giving stern directions, was lost in the confusion. One canoe almost tipped over. I was happy to see how delighted the boys were to be with Greg. He joked with them, and they seemed to find him a jolly companion.

I strolled on up to the main area. There were countless booths, all of them offering various wares. One could buy hot bread, pies, sausages, ribbons, lace, fine carved wood. There were pens of squealing pigs and coops of chickens. A lonely old woman in black sat before gilt cages of green and yellow parakeets. A man with a flushed face sold smoked fish, yelling of their excellent quality to all who passed by his stall. There was a faded orange and pink striped tent where an old Gypsy woman in blue scarves and tarnished gold beads was telling fortunes. Three tired, forlorn looking donkeys were tied outside the tent, their backs laden with carpets and old pots and pans. Nan had rushed directly to this tent, a protesting Billy Johnson dragging along with her.

People yelled greetings, small children darted underfoot, delighting in their day of freedom. But the young men and women of Lockwood dominated the scene. The strong country lads in their best homespun shirts stood together in loud groups, slapping one another on the back and laughing as they eyed the girls, healthy, husky creatures who reminded me of a group of overgrown schoolboys. They seemed to be bursting with energy, eager for the Maypole dance when the girls would choose their partners. By some mutual agreement the boys and girls stayed apart now, sizing each other up and waiting for the dance, when pandemonium would break out. The girls laughed coyly and flitted past the males, swishing their skirts and tossing flaxen blonde curls. They were as eager as the men, longing to feel those strong arms about their waists and to cavort off to secluded spots. The air was electric with all these ready-to-burst emotions.

I purchased a glass of lemonade and found a seat beneath an oak tree. The limbs spread layers of thick purple shade over the grass, the boughs hanging low. It was cool here, and not nearly so noisy as it was a little distance away from the main activity. I could sit here and wait for Greg and watch the bright interplay of color without being a part of it. I watched the carousel as it whirled around, the painted horses bobbing up and down with flushed children holding the reins. Two large Maypoles stood on a brightly green lawn, their long colored ribbons entwined with flowers. Each girl would take a ribbon and dance as the boys darted in and out, the girls wrapping their ribbons around the boy they favored. A huge wooden dance floor was set up nearby. Colored lanterns would be put up at dusk and musicians would play as the couples danced.

I was tired already. We had been here since noon and I had helped Greg with the boys. They were like a pack of noisy puppies, delightful to be with for a while but draining energy. Greg had bought them lollipops and lemonade, much to the disapproval of Mr. Stephenson, and we had taken them to inspect all the booths. I was glad that I could beg off the canoe ride and sit here alone for a little while. I had tried to do as the villagers and put aside all cares, but I could not shake off the intense anger and alarm I had felt upon reading the note, knowing as I did that Roderick Mellory had sent it. Nor could I forget the insult of the dress. Both things bothered me still, and I was irritated with myself for letting them put me in such a state.

"Miss Todd, isn't it?"

I must have been lost in thought, for I had not heard anyone approaching the tree. Paul Mellory had come up from behind, wheeling his chair silently. He sat there gazing at me with melancholy brown eyes, a lock of brown hair fallen across his forehead. There was a green and blue plaid rug over his knees and a slender book of poetry in his lap. I did not know how long he might have been there contemplating me as I thought about his brother.

"You—you startled me," I said.

"I have that ability," he said bitterly. "Startling people, you know." He looked down at his concealed legs, his thin lips grimacing. He was a handsome boy, perhaps a year or two older than I, but the bitter lines and the shadowy eyes were those of one much older.

"It is Miss Angela Todd, isn't it?" he asked.

"Yes," I replied.

"I saw you at church Sunday. You saw me, too."

I blushed. I could feel the color staining my cheeks.

"I did not intend to stare," I said, remembering the hate-filled look he had given me as the Mellorys' carriage drove away.

"I am quite accustomed to having people stare," he said, "which is one of the primary reasons I seldom go out. I'm here today only to indulge my sister. She thinks I should get out more, meet more people. Ordinarily, she is a very sensible young woman."

He spoke in a hard, sharp voice, enunciating each word as though it were hated. All the while he talked his dark brown eyes examined me as though I were an unusual specimen, a butterfly that he had impaled on a board.

"The fresh air will do me good, she says," Paul Mellory said. "I suppose it can't hurt me."

"Is your sister here?"

"Yes, Laurel wanted to come. She wants to buy some lace and some material—probably some bracelets and beads and ribbons, too. But she has so little opportunity to indulge in such foolish, feminine things."

"You consider such things foolish?" I asked.

"I consider most of life foolish."

"Then I pity you," I replied.

"I am accustomed to pity, too."

"You're not a very pleasant person, Mr. Mellory."

"Should I be"—he pointed to his legs—"with this?"

"I'm sure you find it convenient."

"Convenient, Miss Todd?"

"It gives you something to hide behind. Because you are crippled, you can sneer at people, and life, and justify yourself in doing so. It gives you an excuse for being so unpleasant."

"You're quite the little thinker," he said.

"No, I just see what's before my eyes."

He smiled bitterly, but the look in his dark brown eyes changed. There had been active dislike before, but now there was something almost like admiration. At least there was an active interest, whereas there had been only disdain previously. Perhaps in insulting the man I had touched some hidden spring, had drawn him out of his obsessive self-pity. The smile flickered on his lips and died.

"You don't find life intolerable?" he asked.

"Why should I?"

"Because it is."

"Not from where I stand, Mr. Mellory."

"I suppose you're one of those active little do-gooders, like my sister, full of sunshine and always ready to find the bright side of things."

"That sounds loathsome," I said, "and not like me at all. I am afraid I am primarily interested in Miss Angela Todd, although I find the rest of the world interesting, too."

He spread his hands out, encompassing the fair grounds and all the people thronging about it. "Look at this," he said, "you don't find it a disgusting spectacle? Sober, hard working people throwing away money they don't have, acting like children. And later on it becomes even worse. It's like a primeval mating ceremony, those Maypoles, those young people dancing in the most scandalous manner. . . ." He fell into silence, contemplating this as though it was hard to conceive.

I said nothing. I sensed the reason why Paul Mellory felt harshly about the May Day Fete. He could never dance and be caught up in a flower-garlanded ribbon, could never fling his arms about a slender waist and carry a young girl off to a secluded spot. He resented that others could do what he couldn't. He moved suddenly and the book fell out of his lap. I picked it up. It was a copy of the sonnets of Milton. I handed the book to him.

"I find it hard to believe that you can be so bitter about life, Mr. Mellory, and still appreciate the poems of John Milton."

He stuck the book under his rug, as though he was ashamed of it. He glared at me with defiant eyes.

"Poetry is something different," he snapped.

"Poetry is the breath of life."

"How would you know?"

"I am not illiterate, Mr. Mellory."

"You like poetry?" he asked, as though it were inconceivable.

"Very much. And music too. When I lived in London I went to all of the concerts I could afford, and to the theater."

"You are an unusual young woman, Miss Todd. Very unusual. I must confess I was curious about you. I saw you sitting under this tree and I came over solely to find out what kind of woman you were, what kind of woman it took to defy my brother."

"I take it he is not used to being defied?"

"Not at all. When he offered such a nice sum to your lawyer, he was certain Dower House would be in the family again. He had no idea that he would be turned down. It bewildered him."

"Why does he want Dower House so desperately?" I asked.

"It's a fixed idea with him. Phoenix Hall must be maintained in the grand style of the past, and that cannot be done with a stranger living on the premises. Not many men have a purpose in life. Rod does, and he has devoted most of his adult life to it. It almost killed him to see Phoenix Hall slipping: money going out, none coming in, plaster falling in the halls, bricks crumbling, varnish peeling. My father was a wonderful man, but he was a poor manager. He was lax, and he was too kindhearted."

"Can one be too kindhearted?" I asked.

He paused, reflecting. "My father was," he said slowly. "Phoenix Hall suffered for it."

"And now Phoenix Hall prospers and the people suffer."

"You might say that. Rod closed down the quarries. They hated him for that. They had to get out and find some other means of livelihood. They had to use some initiative. Phoenix Hall has been supporting too many of the people for too long a time. Now it doesn't. Now they work on farms and produce more grain and vegetables. Some of them have gone into various trades. Now that they do not rely on Phoenix Hall they are doing more for themselves and for the whole of Lockwood. Ultimately, it will mean a richer Lockwood because my brother refused to go on working the quarries when the demand for granite had ceased."

This was not said with conviction. He said the words as though he was repeating an argument someone else had given.

"That is a philosophical way of justifying it," I replied.

"One must justify it somehow," he said quietly.

I looked up at him sharply. Something about the way he said those last words gave me an insight into his true nature. He was not in accord with his brother. He was a sensitive young man who was considerate of other people, despite his pose to the contrary. Mr. Patterson had told me that Paul Mellory was like his father by nature, and I saw that now, behind all his pretense. He did not want people to see his true nature. It would make them pity him all the more, and it would make him vulnerable to them. He was too proud for that.

"You don't approve of what your brother did?" I asked.

"I did not say that, Miss Todd."

"But you implied it. You would not have put the people out of work if you had been in charge. You really don't approve of your brother at all, do you?"

"But he is my brother, Miss Todd."

"And you are loyal. I admire that."

"I respect him for his ability to accomplish what he sets out to accomplish. I admire his ability to let nothing stand in his way, to achieve his goals no matter what the odds against him."

"And I am in his way now?"

"It would seem so."

I smiled to myself. I brushed bits of grass from my sapphire blue skirt and accidently exposed a ruffle of my fine lace petticoat. A ray of sunlight slanted through the overhanging limbs of the tree, touching my lustrous brown hair. I could see Paul Mellory looking at me with admiration. The conversation had stimulated me, and I was flushed, my eyes sparkling.

"It would appear that my brother has met a worthy opponent," Paul Mellory said.

"Thank you, Paul," I replied.

The name had come to my lips instinctively, and I had already spoken it before realizing my error. He looked up, pleased. I felt his friendliness then, and I knew that I had won him over. He would be my friend regardless of what happened between his brother and me. That was satisfying to know.

"I am very sorry about the incident the other day," Paul said. "My brother told me what happened, although he told Laurel merely that you had stumbled over a piece of lumber. Both of us were concerned. Laurel wanted to go to Dower House the next morning and take some broth and see if you were all right, but Rod wouldn't let her."

I was touched by his sister's concern, but I could see why Roderick Mellory did not want her to know exactly what happened.

"My brother was greatly upset over the matter," Paul continued. "He discharged the men immediately. He was quite brutal about it, would not give them their wages and threatened to beat them to a pulp if ever they showed their faces in this neighborhood again. The men were brutes. It is in their nature. I hope that this will not sour you on Phoenix Hall completely, Miss Todd."

His voice became suddenly much younger, suddenly very sincere. "I hope you will come to see us quite often," he said, hesitating just a little. "I—I would enjoy that. There are so few interesting people around here, people you can talk to, I would like very much to be able to talk to you more. You like music. Perhaps I could play for you."

"I would enjoy that, Paul."

"Here comes my sister," he said. "Don't mention any of this, Miss Todd. She doesn't know what happened."

"Of course I won't mention it."

Laurel Mellory came up to us, walking in the springing, lilting way of a person very young,

very exciting. She was wearing a pink and powder blue striped dress, and the skirt swirled as she
walked. Silvery blonde hair bounced about her
shoulders. There was a faint pink flush on her
cheeks. Her dark blue eyes were alive with excitement. I thought she looked too intense, too animated, as though she was not used to as much
excitement as she had had today. There was still
something very sad about the girl, for all her animation.

"See, Paul!" she cried, holding out a bracelet of
dangling gold bangles, "I bought this from the
Gypsy woman. She told my fortune, too. And this
lace"—she held out a bolt of the exquisite stuff—
"it is the very finest, and quite expensive, but it
will be lovely on my petticoats. I had a huge sausage rolled in bread, and some candy." She was
chattering like a child let out on holiday after
months of dreary imprisonment. Paul listened to
her as one would listen to a child, letting them
prattle on, not really paying any attention.

Laurel Mellory saw me, and she became very
quiet. I saw that her face was lined with fatigue.
The curious blue stain was still about her eyelids,
giving that haunting look, and the animation died
away, leaving a pale, tired face marked with sadness.

"You are Miss Angela Todd, aren't you?" she
asked.

I nodded, smiling. She smiled, too, a faint
smile.

"I meant to come visit you after your accident.
Something came up, and I didn't get to come. I
had some chicken broth."

"I appreciate your concern," I said.

"It is nice to see that you are all right. I have

wanted so to meet you. I knew your aunt. You've been making friends with Paul? I am glad. I do hope we can be friends, too."

"We had better go, Laurel," Paul Mellory said. "You look tired. I have had enough."

"Oh, but I so wanted to see the Maypole Dance," Laurel protested.

"You're overstimulated as it is. You know how you have to pay for these excitements. Days in bed, cold cloths on your head, nerves. You mustn't make it worse. Roderick will be displeased."

"Yes," Laurel said, very quietly. "We must go. We must not let our brother be displeased." She turned to me, unsmiling. "It has been nice meeting you, Miss Todd. I hope we will see each other again soon."

"I hope so, too, Miss Mellory."

Paul Mellory exchanged glances with me. I felt that we had some secret understanding between us. Laurel tucked the rug tightly about his knees, fussing over him as though he were a child, then got behind the chair to push him to their carriage. The lock of hair was still on his tanned forehead, and the dark brown eyes were secretive now, uncommunicative. He did not look back as his sister pushed the wheelchair away. I watched until they vanished around the corner of a tent, wondering about this strange couple and the life they must lead at Phoenix Hall.

Greg came to find me, surrounded by his flock of schoolboys. He was as excited as they were, and it was plain to see that he had enjoyed the canoe rides equally as well. Mr. Stephenson had decided to rest for a while, and Greg had promised to let them all ride the carousel before they left the grounds. It was already getting late, and soon the Maypole Dance would begin. Both Greg and Mr. Stephenson felt the boys should leave before that took place. The boys flittered around Greg like a flock of sparrows in their little brown suits, tugging at his hand, asking him questions, urging him to hurry and put them on the carousel. He smiled at me over all this and together we took the boys to the carousel and put each one on a brightly painted horse.

The calliope music was bright and gay. The horses went bobbing around rapidly, faster and faster. Greg and I stood watching, and he held my hand, almost unconsciously. He had taken it naturally as though it were the expected thing, and I felt his fingers tighten on mine as we watched the boys. He was laughing at their antics, and I watched his face. His gray eyes with their specks of green were full of boyish delight. He might be dissatisfied with his lot as a teacher, I thought, but he was certainly enthusiastic about it, doing his job with relish and commanding the love and respect of his young students. I pulled my hand away as Mr. Stephenson came to join us.

The carousel was slowing down. The boys were emitting loud groans of disappointment, knowing that their day of fun was coming to an end. The calliope music became jerky, spasmodic, then blurted to a stop as the horses jerked to a standstill. The boys climbed off reluctantly and Mr. Stephenson helped Greg herd them all together.

"We'll take them back to school," Greg said. "I can come back in a little while, after we see that they're all fed and put to rest. Will you wait for me, Angela?"

"Yes. I want to see if I can find Nan. You'll be back in time for the dance?"

"Or shortly thereafter."

"I'd hate for you to miss it," I said.

He grinned. "I've seen a dozen of them. All this is new for you, but the first excitement has long since rubbed away for me."

He left, helping his colleague escort the by now dejected boys off the fairgrounds and back to their dormitory rooms at the school. I began to look for Nan. I had caught glimpses of her off and on all day, but I had not talked to her since she darted away to the fortune-teller's tent with Billy. I saw Billy now, leaning against a tree trunk and looking surly and morose. He wore rust-colored trousers and scuffed, dusty brown boots. His coarse linen shirt had enormous gathered sleeves, and there was leather lacing at the throat in lieu of buttons. His handsome face was uncharacteristically grim, the mouth turned down at the corner and the penny-colored eyes flat and hard. I imagined that he and Nan had had one of their spectacular quarrels.

"Where is Nan, Billy?" I asked.

"You'll have to ask Dereck Miller about that," he snapped.

"Dereck Miller? Who is he?"

"Your Nan can tell you all about *him.*"

"Oh, dear—"

"Me, I'm havin' nothing more to do with her."

I left him leaning against the tree trunk, scowling bitterly over my minx of a maid. I found Nan a little later. She was at one of the booths, accepting a piece of cake held out to her in the palm of a boy who must be Dereck Miller. He was extremely tall, over six foot, with thick, dark blond hair and adoring blue eyes. Several of the Lockwood girls a distance away were eyeing him appreciatively, but he only had eyes for Nan. She took the cake from his palm and nibbled on it. Chocolate crumbs drifted to the ground.

"Nan," I cried, going over to them.

"Oh, Miss Angel! I've got so much to tell you." She turned to the boy, dismissing him. "See you at the dance. Don't forget to jump in front of my ribbon. There, he's gone. Isn't he lovely, Miss Angel? Did you see those arms. He pitches hay. That develops the muscles. And he has such sweet eyes. He's dumb, of course, like all these lads, but beautiful nevertheless."

"What happened between you and Billy?"

"Oh, he's such a lout! He made fun of me for having my fortune told. Then he wouldn't buy those nice red ribbons for my hair. I'm all through with him, Miss Angel. I can tell you that right now."

"You're heartless, Nan."

"I'm tired of his bossiness. Besides, Dereck is so much nicer."

We strolled about the grounds and Nan told me about all the things that had happened to her, spending most of the time extrolling the virtues of her new conquest. I heard the history of Dereck Miller and all about how he won wrestling matches and weight lifting contests and had won a little doll for her at the shooting gallery set up on the grounds here. She looked charming in the green and white striped dress adorned with countless flouncy pink ruffles. She skipped and danced about the fairgrounds like a delighted child, having the time of her life. She told me that Dereck had taught her the steps of the Maypole dance. She was going to dance with the other girls, even though she was not from Lockwood, and she was very excited about that.

The electric air of anticipation had grown stronger now. Most of the children had been sent home. The sun was beginning to stain the sky with scarlet and gold, and a soft blue twilight was thickening. It was almost time for the dance to begin. People began to shuffle around the Maypoles, wanting to get a good position in which to watch. The musicians had come and were tuning their instruments. The colored lanterns had been strung up over the wooden dance floor, suspended from the limbs of the oak trees. The crowd was restless, noisier than before. I saw many more goatskins of wine, and already a few of the older men were walking unsteadily, pushing people out of their way.

I looked around anxiously for Greg. A young man came up to me and asked me if I was Miss Angela Todd. When I nodded he told me that he had a message for me. One of the boys had gotten sick, he said, and Mr. Ingram had asked him to inform me that he would not be able to come back just yet. It would be after dark before he could get away. I was disappointed, as I had wanted to watch the dance with Greg, but there was nothing I could do.

A signal was given and the girls moved to the Maypoles, picking up their designated ribbons. The crowd moved back, clearing the area. Nan pranced among the Lockwood girls and took her ribbon, bowing saucily to the others. She plucked a pink rose from her ribbon and fastened it in her curls. The boys formed circles around the outer edges of the poles, eager to perform their part in the ritual dance. Each girl raised her ribbon up and stood poised, ready to execute the intricate steps of the dance. The music began, a gay, lilting tune, and the girls moved in unison, skipping, dipping, waltzing, twining their ribbons about the tops of the poles.

It was a beautiful dance, I thought, bright, merry, filled with exciting symbolism as the ribbons wrapped the poles and then were unwound so skillfully by the young girls who moved on light feet, keeping perfect time to the music. The girls were all smiling, cheeks flushed pink with excitement, eyes sparkling, skirts sashaying and hair flying as the tempo quickened. Nan danced with great vivacity, keeping step with the best of them. I saw many of the boys watching her. Billy stood on the outskirts of the crowd, still scowling, watching Nan with angry eyes. Dereck Miller stood in place with the rest of the boys who were going to dance.

The music grew louder, wilder, and upon signal the boys began to dance in and out of the circles, leaping in front of the girls and moving back and forth in a highly suggestive manner, executing little jump steps that kept them always just out of reach. The dance took on a lusty, robust quality, sensual and unabashed in its symbolism. I was a little shocked, but the crowd loved it. They shouted catcalls, making lewd suggestions and offering advice to the boys. They roared with delight as the boys eluded the ribbons, taunting the girls and then allowing themselves to be caught. It was a colorful spectacle, healthy, red-blooded young bodies moving rapidly, ribbons flashing in red, blue and green swirls, flowers coming unfastened and dropping in showers of petals on the dancers. The music grew more intense, the dancers whirled faster and faster until it seemed they would drop with exhaustion, and finally each boy and girl were wrapped in rolls of colored ribbon, imprisoned together and in each other's arms as the music stopped. They were panting, swaying together, joyous in their cries of delight. Nan was leaning against Dereck Miller's chest, her arms about his back. He was grinning, holding her very tightly. The crowd applauded with the sound of thunder, and the couples ran off the green together, holding hands, broken ribbons flying from their shoulders.

"Did you enjoy the spectacle, Miss Todd?"

I whirled around. Roderick Mellory was smiling at me. He must not sense my alarm, I thought, and I tried to remain very cool. His dark eyes were filled with amusement, and his lips were curled up in one of those mocking smiles I remembered so well. My cheeks reddened as I realized that he must have been standing there for a long time, watching me and watching my reactions to the primitive dance.

"How long have you been here?" I asked.

"Since shortly after the dance began."

"Spying on me," I snapped.

"Call it that if you like. I was interested to see how you would react to some of our local customs."

"Why?"

"Because I am interested in you, Miss Todd."

"Interested in me? I wonder. I suppose you would like to discover all my weaknesses and shortcomings so that you could use them. I am sure it would please you to find something to use against me."

"You're not very flattering, Miss Todd."

"I certainly can't think of any other reason why you should be interested in me, Mr. Mellory."

"You're not very imaginative, either."

"Should I be?"

"Most young women are."

"I'm not like most young women."

"I'm beginning to see that."

I could think of nothing to say in return. The crowd had dispersed, moving away in various directions. Night was falling fast now and the shadows were thickening. Over the wooden dance floor the soft, hazy lanterns were like splotches of color, moving slightly in the breeze. Many of the couples had disappeared. Some of them strolled around over the fairgrounds, giggling and embracing, and others danced under the lanterns. I had no idea where Nan and her new beau had gone.

"If you'll excuse me, Mr. Mellory, I must go look for my maid."

"Where is your escort? You didn't come alone?"

"Mr. Ingram brought me. He had to take the boys back to school and was detained."

"How unfortunate for Greg. How fortunate for me."

"What do you mean?"

"Surely you realize that you can't run around here alone. This is the one night when things like —the incident at Phoenix Hall are the accepted thing. A woman alone would be inviting such things."

"Are you trying to frighten me?"

"Not particularly. I'm trying to make you see why my company is desirable for you tonight."

"Your company would not be desirable under any circumstances, Mr. Mellory."

His lips turned down in an ugly frown. He gripped my arm. "I am not going to argue with you," he said harshly. "You are the stubbornest young woman I have ever met. So stubborn it is likely to get you into a lot of trouble one of these days."

"Is that a prediction—or a threat?"

"A threat?"

"I got your note, Mr. Mellory."

"Note?" he said. "What note?"

"Surely you aren't going to deny sending it? Last night a man threw a rock through my window. A note was tied around it. It told me to leave Dower House—before it was too late."

"Too late for what?"

"I'm sure you would know more about that than I."

"A man threw it, you say? Did you get a look at him?"

"It was very dark, Mr. Mellory. I couldn't see him clearly enough to determine any features. That should relieve you somewhat. I am sure you could describe him for me in detail."

"You're taking a bit for granted, Miss Todd."

"Am I? Surely you want me to leave Dower House. That would make it easy for you. You're wrong, though. I am not going to leave. I was not frightened. I was not trembling. I was merely angry. No one is going to frighten me away from my home."

"Perhaps you should have been frightened," he said slowly.

"I'm not the type," I snapped.

"I can see that. Will you promise me one thing? Will you let me know if this happens again?"

"I am sure you will know even before I do."

He frowned. He was still holding my arm. The grip had tightened. I felt the fingers biting into my flesh. I could sense the man's anger and I gloried in it. I had the power to make him angry. I could hold my own with him, and that was something not many could say.

"Since you have been more or less forced to spend this time with me," he said, "can't you at least be civil?"

"Why should I be civil to you, Mr. Mellory?"

"Because you are evidently well brought up, for one reason. You might bring some of that good-breeding into play now. We are together at the fair, whether you like it or not. You might smile. You might let me buy you some refreshments."

"No, thank you," I replied.

"Did you get the dress?" he asked, his tone lighter.

"Yes, Mr. Mellory. It is very lovely."

"I am giving a ball as soon as the repairs are done. I will look forward to seeing you there, in the dress. You will be the most stunning woman there."

"Balls are not my sort of thing," I replied, wondering why he even bothered with all this pretense. We were enemies, and I liked it that way. We both knew where we stood, on opposing sides and this pretense of friendliness only clouded the issue.

We had strolled away from the Maypoles and were mingling among a bustling, belligerent crowd. People stared curiously at the Master of Phoenix Hall as he walked along, holding my arm, disdainful of everything about him. I could see the hatred in the eyes of the people as he passed by. One man spat audibly after we had passed, and although I know Roderick Mellory was aware of it he did not even turn around. It was beneath him to even acknowledge the presence of these people. The fairgrounds might as well have been deserted of everyone but the two of us, I thought.

"My brother told me that he met you today," he said. "You made a very good impression on him. On my sister, too. I heard them talking about you. I figured that you would still be here at the fair, so I decided to come see for myself."

"Out of curiosity?"

"To see you again."

"Why?"

"You made quite an impression on me, too."

"Should I feel ecstatic?" I said scornfully.

"You have a barbed tongue, Miss Todd. It's very unpleasant. You won't allow a man to be attentive to you, will you?"

"I have no desire for anyone like you to be attentive to me."

"You do think I'm a devil, don't you?"

"What I think should make no difference to you, Mr. Mellory."

"You think I would stop at nothing to have my way. You think I am unscrupulous enough to send a man to terrorize you, that I would like to frighten you away from Dower House. I find that image of me quite conceivable, I must admit. I've been called ruthless, and rightly so in many cases, but I do not prey on defenseless women."

His voice sounded sincere and almost a little hurt that I should harbor such thoughts about him. I was not deceived. He was a clever man, shrewd and wily, and I had no doubt that he was an accomplished actor as well. We strolled along slowly, his fingers still gripping my arm. It was completely dark now. Many of the stalls were lighted, and people were still buying food and drink and occasional trinkets. A lad with a rifle was shooting targets at one stall, and his smiling girl stood nearby, her eyes on a gaudy doll she hoped to have won for her.

There was a loud commotion in front of one tent. A crowd of people stood around, eagerly anticipating a fight. I heard loud voices. As we came nearer I saw a head of tarnished golden curls and two men standing face-to-face, stamping the ground for all the world like two bulls head-on, snorting at each other.

"My heavens!" I cried, pulling away from Roderick Mellory. "My maid! She's in the middle of that. I'm afraid they're going to fight over her."

I ran to the edge of the crowd, standing on tiptoe to get a better look. Nan was perched on the counter of the stall, her eyes very wide, very blue. Billy Johnson and Dereck Miller were shouting, both of them red-faced with anger, the muscles of their necks standing out in cords from the strain. The crowd shouted encouragement, and Dereck shoved Billy away from him with such force that Billy fell against one of the men in the crowd. He recovered himself, his eyes filled with murderous hatred. He drew back, doubling up his fists, and the fight was on.

The two men flew at each other, fists flying. Billy knocked his opponent to the ground, leaping on top of him. They grappled, rolling over and over. The crowd roared, moving closer. Nan jumped up on the counter, her heels tapping in excitement as the men fought for her favors. The men thrashed on the ground, almost hidden by clouds of dust. Billy had his arm wrapped around Dereck's throat, straining all his strength into the deadly stranglehold. Dereck's face was red, his eyes bulging. He kicked his legs, fighting furiously to break the hold. His palm was spread over Billy's face, the fingers gouging his eyes.

Dereck managed to break free. He leaped to his feet, kicking at the man still on the ground. Billy groaned as the boot made contact. He grabbed the foot and jerked. Dereck fell backwards, his tall body hitting the ground with great force. It knocked the wind out of him. I gasped in horror, my hand flying to my mouth. Nan danced on the counter, screaming in delight and horror. Roderick Mellory came up beside me. He could not have cared less about the fight. His eyes were on my face. He was smiling grimly.

"Can't you stop them!" I cried.

"I see no reason why I should."

"But they'll kill each other!"

"Hardly. This is merely a form of traditional exercise. They are merely releasing energy. There will be many more fights before this is all over."

"You won't stop it! Then I will—"

I started forward, calling Billy's name. Roderick Mellory caught my arm, pulling me back violently. "Don't be a fool," he said. I was furious, and tears of anger brimmed on my lashes. His lips curled and his dark eyes darted with amusement. He was enjoying this. He was enjoying seeing me distressed. I pounded my fists on his chest in frustration, but his hold on my arm only tightened. I winced in pain. The crowd yelled, Nan screamed, there was the loud noise of blows as fist made contact with flesh.

There was nothing I could do. I stood in silent frustration. Roderick Mellory arched a dark brow as he saw my look of defeat. He curled his arm about my shoulders casually and began to watch the fight with some interest. I stood dumbly, my mind whirling with thoughts. No one paid the slightest attention to the Master of Phoenix Hall now, too engrossed in the fight to pay him any notice.

Both men were on their feet, staggering. Dereck had Billy's arm twisted behind his back, and he wrenched it up between his shoulderblades. I could see the sweat on Billy's forehead, see his eyes close tightly with pain. He reached up and got his fingers in Dereck's blond hair. He jerked with all his might and almost snapped Dereck's neck as he pulled. Dereck lost his hold and went flying around. Billy slammed his fist against the side of Dereck's head, and blood spurted. Dereck drove his fist into Billy's stomach. Billy doubled up and almost fell over. They were both covered with dust now and Billy's eye was swollen and already beginning to discolor.

"Hit him again!" a man shouted lustily.

"Knock him over!" another cried.

"Don't let him get behind you!"

"Shove! Get his throat! Watch it, he's moving around!"

The uproar was deafening. The crowd jumped and pounded each other on the back in their excitement. Nan had covered her face in mock horror, but she peeked between her fingers, watching. She was the heroine of this bloody drama, and the role thrilled her. I could see her intense pleasure as she skipped along the top of the counter, swishing her skirts and tapping her heels.

The men were standing apart now, both stunned, both almost at the end of their strength. Their chests heaved, their faces glistened with sweat. Dereck was staggering, his blond hair over his forehead. Billy stood with his legs planted wide apart, his arms hanging at his side. Dereck stumbled forward. Billy doubled his fist and swung back his arm, waved it in a wide arc and smashed his fist against the jaw of his opponent. There was a splintering noise like a bone cracking. A great sigh rose from the crowd as Dereck sank to his knees. His eyes had a stunned look. He fell back, sprawled on the ground, out. Billy stood for a moment, panting, then he flung out his arm and swept Nan off the counter, pulling her down into his arms.

Nan laid her head on his shoulder and he wrapped an arm about her. They stood silently, the defeated man sprawled out at their feet. Nan took a handkerchief and wiped the dust from Billy's face, touched the discolored eye with gentle fingers and made little clucking noises. The crowd broke up, looking for fresh excitements to satisfy their robust, primitive appetites. There would be other fights. There would be loud shouts and straining muscles and spurting blood.

I felt ill. Roderick Mellory still had his arm about my shoulders and I pulled away. He grinned. He looked cool and disdainful in his black suit. None of the excitement of the fight had been communicated to him. He might have been standing on a riverbank, watching the water flowing, for all the effect the fight had had on him. I stared at his face, wondering how such a man could live with himself. It seemed that nothing touched him, nothing ruffled that cool, calm exterior. He was maddeningly self-possessed. I wondered what it would take to crack that exterior. What would it take to pierce that armor and reach the man inside? I turned away, upset and bewildered by all that had happened.

Nan and Billy wandered off, their arms entwined. Someone helped Dereck Miller to his feet and led him away. I heard the music playing, saw the hazy colored lights over the dance floor. My head was swimming. There had been too many impressions, too many emotions, too quickly. I bit my lower lip, trying to keep control of myself.

"Come," Roderick Mellory said. "I am going to buy you a glass of cold cider. You need it."

I offered no protest as he led me away. He bought the drink. Then he led me to a seat beneath an arbor. The lattice was completely covered with thick green vines, making it a retreat from the crowd. I sat quietly, drinking the tart, cold cider, and Roderick Mellory stood with his hands resting on the lattice, breathing quietly and respecting my silence. Here on the outskirts of the grounds I could see fireflies as they flew among the dark shrubs, making soft yellow lights that flickered for a moment and then died away. Behind us, in the wooded areas, we could hear people moving, scuffling, laughing.

I felt exhausted and depressed, too tired even to argue with the man who stood over me. I hadn't the energy for quick retorts. I hadn't even the energy to hate him or to resent his presence.

"What kind of man are you?" I asked quietly.

"A very simple man," he replied.

"Simple? I can hardly see that."

"Quite simple. A man with one purpose. One clear cut goal in my life. One goal to strive for, one thought foremost in my mind. That's very simple, isn't it?"

"Why does Phoenix Hall mean so much to you?"

"It is mine. It is permanent. It stands for all I stand for. The house has been ours for hundreds of years. I want to keep it. I want it to be what it was. So many families have lost their estates, have been reduced to genteel poverty, to charity even. I will not let that happen to the Mellorys."

"I can understand that," I replied. "But—it seems so empty, so lonely, to have—just that one thing."

He laughed softly. "You think I should have a wife? You think I should have children and burdens and responsibilities and obligations?" He shook his head. "Romance, Miss Todd. Romantic drivel. When I have done all I need to do to Phoenix Hall, then I'll look for those things you fancy I should have. I want a son to carry on, of course, and I shall have one, eventually. I'll bring him up to think the way I think, to respect the things I respect."

"And your wife?"

"She will be chosen carefully. She will have all the qualities that are suitable for the Mistress of Phoenix Hall. She will know her place, and she will fulfill the role I have appointed her."

"And will she be happy? Will you be happy?"

"Happiness is a relative thing, Miss Todd. It is not a state of romantic blissfulness. It is the achievement of something, the knowledge that you have done what you set out to do."

"It all sounds so cold and bloodless," I remarked, "this plan of yours. I do not envy you. I certainly do not envy your future wife as you describe her. You've left out all emotion, all feeling."

"I am not an emotional man, Miss Todd. I have seen what emotional excess can lead to. I'm safely out of that now."

I knew that he was speaking of his youth, being thrown out of Oxford and, later on, the romantic entanglement in London, the lady with the blonde hair, the duel in Hyde Park. He must have been a rake then, a dashing, daring, hot-blooded creature so different from the man who stood here now, arranging his life in such a methodical manner. I would have preferred the earlier Roderick Mellory, I thought.

"What about you?" he asked. "What are you going to do with your life now that you have Dower House?"

"I am going to—to live there. I'm going to work in the garden. I am going to read. I am going to—to be content."

"That sounds dull. A hermit's life hardly suits a young woman with your temperament."

"A hermit's life is much better than working for a living, having to put up with the whims of others, using thread and needle to make dresses others will wear, worrying about expenses. I had that, and now the life of a hermit will suit me fine."

This sounded very sensible, but I wondered if it was true. For the first time in my adult life I had security, I did not have to worry about money, about making ends meet, but I wondered if this would make up for the things that were so obviously lacking. Perhaps I was fooling myself. The

excitements of the day had left me pensive and
moody, and I thought how strange it was to be
sitting here talking about these things with the
man who was my enemy, the one person with
whom I should never let down my defenses.

At this point, Greg found us in the arbor. He
had a look of concern on his face, thinking that I
might have left already. Roderick Mellory greeted
Greg affably and asked him some inconsequential
questions about teaching. Greg thanked Mellory
for watching after me and then the Master of
Phoenix Hall departed, vanishing into the darkness. Greg wanted to know how Roderick Mellory
and I had come upon each other, and I explained
briefly what had happened, leaving out all personal references and making it sound very casual.
Greg seemed to be satisfied with this, and I was
relieved when he began to talk about the child
who had been sick. We talked for a while, and
finally Greg led me to the dance floor.

I was too tired to enjoy dancing. I had to force
myself to move in step with the music, to smile
and pretend interest in Greg's remarks. He held
his arm tightly about my waist and swirled me
around the colored lights, not noticing my list-
lessness. His face was animated in its pleasure,
and he danced as briskly and with as much enjoy-
ment as the hearty young couples who crowded
the floor. I saw Nan dancing with Billy Johnson.
Her head was thrown back, her face as open and
glowing as a flower as she looked into his eyes.
Billy's eye was blue now, with purple edges, and
there was a bruise on the side of his head, but he
danced with as lively a step as any of the other
lads. The music played on and on, merry, bright.

Boots stomped and girls laughed and all were moved by the festive air.

Later, Greg and I stood in the darkness of an open field, waiting with hundreds of others for the fireworks display. Greg held my hand. I stood very close to him, my body drained of all energy, and yet the tiredness was almost comfortable now. I felt serene and secure, standing there so near Greg, his hand clasping mine tightly. People talked quietly, waiting for the first burst of color that would lighten the solid black sky. Ohs and ahs filled the air when the first sizzle of burning wick sounded like a hissing snake and the rocket shot up in a stream of flame, softly exploding high in the sky and showering with a million pink and gold sparks that slowly drifted down and died. There were feathery blue and green explosions, silver and red bursts, purple and violet showers, all coloring the night with incredible beauty. The crowd was silent, awed and respectful of this miracle, and when the sky was black once more, May Day was officially over.

I was sleepy on the way home. The horses moved slowly, clopping heavy hooves on the road. Greg held the reins in one hand, and his arm enfolded my shoulder. We did not talk. My eyelids were heavy, and I laid my head on his shoulder, too sleepy to make any pretense of sociability. The movement of the carriage lulled me to sleep. Today had been too full, too active, and it was a relief to just close my eyes and not try to think of all that had happened.

7

*L*aurel Mellory came to see me frequently in the weeks that followed. I helped her trim her petticoats with the lace she had bought at the fair and we sat in the parlor, talking quietly as I trimmed the fine linen with the delicate cobwebby lace. I came to know the girl and her many moods. She had frail health and was subject to severe migraine headaches and burning fevers, and when these came she had to stay in bed with all the draperies tightly drawn. With me she was bright and bubbling with gaity and then, for no apparent reason, sunk into a fit of melancholy gloom.

She told me of all that was happening at Phoenix Hall. The outside repairs had been completed and the workmen sent back to Devon, and now Roderick Mellory was having work done inside. A fine craftsman from Paris had come to work on the wainscoting, and an Italian with an impressive reputation was working with marble. The parquet floor of the ballroom had been touched up, the plaster redone, new paint added. It would all be completed near the end of the month, and then there was to be a great ball to display a renovated Phoenix Hall. The expense of it all was staggering, but Roderick Mellory would be satisfied.

"All the money he made in India is gone," Laurel said, "but the house is beautiful. I wonder what will happen now."

"What do you mean?" I asked.

"Now that it is all done, Roderick will have nothing to do. There has to be something to fill his hours. He can't stand to be idle. I am worried."

I had no doubt that Roderick Mellory would find some way to fill his hours. When the repairs were all done he could devote more time to trying to evict me from Dower House. After I had told him about the note thrown through my window, there had been no more incidents, although Nan swore she saw a man prowling out in the garden. She had awakened me, alarmed, but when we peered outside no one was there. I thought I saw a dim light flashing in the granite quarries, but it came and went so quickly that I could have been mistaken.

"Did you see a light out there?" I asked Nan. "In the quarry?"

"Not this time," Nan said.

"What do you mean?"

"It's been there before, Miss Angel. I have seen lights out there, moving around. Sometimes more than one."

"Perhaps it's a farmer, looking for a stray animal," I suggested.

"If it is, then those animals sure get loose a lot," Nan said. "Do you think that's what it is?"

"Probably, Nan."

I remembered Billy Johnson telling us about the lights in the quarry and in the woods and the local speculation that the band of robbers had a den hereabouts. I remembered the highwayman dressed all in black and the two stocky brutes with him. That seemed such a long time ago, and it was fantastic to believe that they could be somewhere around here. Billy had told us that the quarries had numerous caves and tunnels and places where the bandits could hide and store their loot, but if that was so why was it that they had never been discovered? The quarries had been searched a number of times. I felt that all this talk was just that, simply talk. It was certainly nothing for me to worry about.

I thought no more about it until one night when we were sitting out in the garden. It was warm and the lilac tree filled the air with heavy perfume. We had been sitting here in the old wicker chairs, watching as the sun went down in a burst of scarlet flame. As the shadows thickened, we continued to sit and talk idly about the day's events. Night fell and a few frosty stars glimmered behind dark clouds. We could hear a cricket chirping under the back step and the boughs of the trees groand a little in the breeze. Peter lay at my feet, sleeping. A few fireflies circled in the shrubs, piercing the darkness occasionally with yellow glow. Nan and I fell silent, both of us very weary and yet enjoying the peace and beauty of the garden at night.

When I first saw the light, I thought it was a firefly. It moved in the granite quarry, far away, a very dim light. I watched for a moment thinking perhaps it would go away, but the light was still there, moving steadily, as though a man was walking with a hooded lantern. Then there was another light, moving towards the first one, as though two men were meeting in the quarry to discuss some secret business. I thought I could hear voices from far away.

"Do you see that?" I whispered to Nan.

"Where?"

"Over there—in the quarry."

"Those lights again," Nan said. "I told you I'd seen 'em."

"What would anyone be doing in the granite quarries at night?" I was not alarmed, but I was very curious.

"I don't like it, Miss Angel," Nan said, "not a bit. There's not anyone else around here for miles, except for the folks at Phoenix Hall. It's peculiar —those lights."

"Look—they've disappeared," I said.

"Where did they go? It's like they were swallowed up."

"I don't know, Nan. It's curious."

I did not sleep well that night. I kept imagining noises in the house. Every creak of the floorboard, every flurry of wind through a crack, seemed to be magnified. I awoke once, certain that I had heard something down in the cellar, but Peter had not barked and Nan had not awakened so I tried to convince myself that it was all my imagination.

Greg came to see me the next day, and when I told him about the lights in the quarry he laughed and said I must have imagined them. I asked if he had heard the talk about the highwaymen having a den in this area, and he agreed with me that it was simply talk. The people around here thrived on rumors, he explained. There was so little excitement ordinarily that they invented stories to add color to the dullness. The highwaymen would be far too clever to work from one specific location. It was more likely that they roamed around like a band of Gypsies.

"But they always attack in this part of the country," I said.

"All over Cornwall," he replied. "That covers a lot of country."

"And none of their loot has ever been recovered. They must have hidden it somewhere."

"More likely it's all gone out of the country," Greg replied.

"It's curious that they have never been caught."

"The leader is evidently quite intelligent," Greg said. "They do not have any system that could trap them by its regularity. Months may pass and there will be no holdups, and then there may be as many as three or four in a month. No, they're clever. Very clever."

"Greg, they say the leader is someone from Lockwood, or at least someone who has connections here. Do you think that's possible?"

"Anything is possible, Angela. But I don't think it likely. It is unfortunate that you had to have the experience you did. It's made you overly sensitive to all these rumors. It is lucky you weren't harmed. Those men must be treacherous."

"The leader was—almost polite."

"Polite?"

"At least I thought so. He had breeding."

Greg threw his head and laughed. It was a rich, pleasant sound. His eyes danced with amusement. "A well bred highwayman," he said. "That amuses me, Angela. That's an observation that could only be made by some very young woman who reads too many novels."

"Just the same, it's so."

He smiled, placing his hand on my arm. "Let's talk about something besides bandits," he said. "Roderick Mellory's ball is to be held on the fifth of April. You'll receive an invitation. I want you to go with me. It will be the grand event in this part of the country."

"I'm not so sure I want to go," I said.

"Why not?"

"I don't like Roderick Mellory. I don't want to go to Phoenix Hall."

"Very few people like him," Greg replied, smiling, "but that's not any reason for turning down an invitation to his ball. It will be glamorous. You'll meet all the gentry from a hundred miles around. None of them like Mellory, either, but they'll jump at the chance to see his house and eat his food and drink his champagne."

"I *am* curious," I admitted, "and Laurel would like for me to come."

"Then you'll go?"

I nodded. "I'm curious to see what Roderick Mellory thinks is grand. I am sure it will all be rather tasteless."

"Never underestimate Rod. He can be charming when he pleases, and he will be at his best for this thing. It will be the first entertainment he has given at Phoenix Hall since he inherited it. I'm sure it'll be worth seeing."

"I'm certain of that, too."

Greg left, and I spent the rest of the afternoon working in the garden. Now that May was half gone, the plants and flowers were blooming in profusion and required much of my time. I enjoyed being on my hands and knees, working in the rich, loamy soil. I liked digging my hands in the earth and pulling out the hard roots of the herbs. I had learned the name for each of them and knew their properties and how to care for them. Working in the garden was a joy to me, and that afternoon I worked until the sun was beginning to sink and stain the sky with dark golden banners. One of the roots was obstinate and I couldn't pull it up. I looked around for my spade but couldn't find it. It was not among the leaves nor could I find it on the grass. I was determined to get the root up before I went in for the evening.

I vaguely remembered seeing a rusty old spade in the cellar. It would do as well, so I decided to go get it. The sun was sinking fast, dying in a glory of dark gold on the darkening blue sky, and shadows were beginning to lengthen in the yard as I walked inside. Nan and Billy had gone for a stroll, and the house was empty. It seemed very still and silent as I went into the kitchen and unlocked the lock we had put on the cellar door. I left the door wide open to give enough light to see by. I had put aside my first aversion to the cellar, but the same nasty odor rose to my nostrils as I went down the damp steps.

The floor was damp, too, and we had done nothing about the disorder. We had merely added to it by sending down more trunks and boxes. Billy had brought down several of these, along with several pieces of furniture. As I searched for the spade, my head brushed against a cobweb and I felt it stick to my hair in silky threads. I brushed it away, irritated. There was just enough light for me to see dim outlines, and I could not locate the spade. The walls of the shelves seemed to loom up, very dark. Trunks and boxes cluttered the floor. They were covered with dirt and dust and mildew had spotted the lid of one of the old brass-bound leather trunks. The place was filthy, the air was stale and laden with unpleasant odors. I stumbled against a box, hitting my knee sharply on it. I gasped, reaching down to rub my knee. It was then that I noticed the spade. It had been kicked into a corner, and as I moved to get it I saw something else that stopped me.

There were fresh footprints, heavy ones, pressed firmly into the hard, damp earth of the floor. The light was not good, but I could see the outlines of heavy boots, several perfect boot-shaped imprints on the floor. I knelt down to examine them, a little alarmed. I couldn't tell too much about them, but I knew that they should not be here. I felt the imprints, running my fingers over them. They were large and deep. Whoever had made them was a large man, heavy. I bit my lower lip, suddenly frightened. The cellar was almost dark, what light there was coming from the opened door gradually fading. The house was empty. I was alone. I thought about the crash we had heard that first night in Dower House. I remembered the noises I had imagined I heard last night, and I remembered the strange lights in the quarry. My heart began to pound, and for a moment I was paralyzed, unable to move from where I knelt.

Then I saw the large, wide rut, as though something heavy had been shoved or pulled across the floor. I stood up, relieved. How foolish of me to have been alarmed, I thought. Billy had probably been down here recently, fetching something for Nan, a jar of preserves, a bottle of pickles, and had had to move a trunk in order to get to it. This cellar seemed to bring out the worst in me, causing me to imagine all sorts of dark, mysterious things. The place was dark and dirty and had a nasty odor, but that was no reason for me to let it work on my nerves and cause these ugly fancies. I got the spade and went upstairs, resolving to give the cellar a thorough cleaning and forget all this foolishness.

Nan and Billy came in a little later, both of them radiant with good nature, poking each other playfully and laughing at some private joke. Billy's eye was almost healed now, the flesh about it a light mauve. Ever since his fight with Dereck Miller he and Nan had seemed closer and didn't quarrel nearly so much. Nan was not so bossy, and I thought Billy walked with an extra swing to his shoulders. He seemed more possessive and masterful, and Nan seemed to delight in this change in their relationship. I asked Billy if he had been down in the cellar recently.

"I took some trunks and things down a couple of weeks ago," he said.

"But you haven't been down since then—perhaps to get a jar of pickles or something?"

"No, Miss Angela, I sure haven't."

"Why do you ask?" Nan inquired, her face full of curiosity.

"No—no reason. I merely wondered," I said.

I left them in the kitchen. Nan had decided that she wanted to bake some fresh bread and she was in a flurry of taking down bowls, sifting the flour, having Billy stoke the stove and light the oven. I went into the parlor and took up my basket of sewing. Billy hadn't been in the cellar in two weeks. Someone had been there. Who? How did they get in? What in the world were they doing down there? No, I told myself, you can't start this. There is a logical explanation for the footprints. They might be old ones. The light wasn't good. You imagined they were fresh. Billy is the only one who has been down there. They are his footprints. They have to be his. I tried to reason with myself and still the alarm I felt growing in my mind. Nothing was wrong in the cellar. I kept telling myself that, and after a while I was convinced that it was true.

May was almost over now as Nan and I sat in the parlor, two weeks after I had discovered the footprints in the cellar. I had never told Nan about them, not wanting her to be alarmed, and I had almost forgotten them myself with all the activity that had taken place since. Roderick Mellory's ball would be held quite soon now. I had received an engraved invitation with a little note at the bottom in his handwriting. It said he looked forward to seeing me in the dress he had sent. I was not going to give him that satisfaction. I had ordered bolts of red and amethyst colored satin, and Nan and I were going to make the gown I would wear. It would not be as spectacular as the one Roderick Mellory had sent, but I had a Parisian pattern I would make it by, and I felt it would be as lovely in its way and far more suitable.

Nan sat in the chair with her lap covered with the richly textured material. She was sewing fine, tiny stitches in the bodice. A roll of glossy amethyst velvet ribbon was curled on the arm of the chair, a pair of scissors and a box of thread at her feet. The tissue paper pieces of pattern were scattered about the floor. Peter sniffed at a piece before curling up on the hearth rug. Nan's canary was asleep in its cage. The late afternoon sun came through the window.

"Is Mr. Ingram coming by this afternoon?" Nan asked.

"I think so. He's going to bring a book I want to read."

"He's been coming to see you an awful lot, Miss Angel."

"Do you think so?" I asked, not really paying attention to her.

"Yes. Wait until he sees you in this gown. That will do it. It's going to be the most beautiful gown in the world, and when you wear it you'll look like a princess. Mr. Ingram will be helpless."

"You're talking nonsense, Nan," I replied. "Mr. Ingram and I are merely friends, nothing more."

"This gown might help to change that. It's cut very low . . ."

"Be quiet," I said. "I'm trying to concentrate."

I sat at the old antique desk, trying to compose a letter in reply to one Mr. Patterson had sent to me. He had invested some of my money and it had already brought in a small profit. He wanted to know if I wanted the rest of it invested in the same manner. I knew little about such matters, but I was going to let him invest some more of the inherited money. I had no head for figures or business details, and it was difficult to write such a letter. My mind kept wandering. I looked down at the fine cream-colored paper, touched the watermark with my fingertip, stuck the nib of my pen in my mouth, thinking of how the letter should be worded. The surface of the desk was cluttered. There was a large green felt blotter, a black onyx pen set, a bronze paperweight in the shape of a lion's head. An oil lamp with a green glass shade helped me to see. I put the pen aside and folded up the paper in disgust, deciding to finish the letter at another time.

I opened one of the bottom drawers to put the pen away. As I tried to close it, it jammed. I pushed hard, trying to get it shut, but it would not move. I shoved hard with both hands and the drawer slammed. I heard a tiny click, as though a spring had been touched, and I was startled to see the bottom panel of the desk fly back and a small drawer slide out. I had not known of its existence, thinking the wood was solid there. I pulled the drawer open, extremely curious.

There were several notebooks with limp leather bindings, the pages rather yellowed. There was also a gun. It was a small pistol with a varnished wooden handle inlaid with pearl. I picked it up and examined it. It was very old, the metal nicked in a couple of places. It fit perfectly in the palm of my hand.

"Look, Nan," I said. "A secret drawer. There are a lot of notebooks and this gun."

"My goodness," Nan said. "We went through that desk and we didn't see any of these things."

"The drawer flew open when I shoved in the bottom one. There must be a spring that releases it."

"I wonder who the gun belonged to?"

"It must have been my aunt's," I replied. "Look, there's a key, too."

The key was large and made of tarnished brass. It did not look like it would fit any of the doors at

Dower House, and I wondered why my aunt had kept it here in this secret drawer with the gun and notebooks. "How strange," I said, turning it over in my hand. "I wonder what it fits." Nan leaned over my shoulder, intrigued by the secret drawer.

"Maybe the notebooks will give us a clue," Nan said.

They were no help at all. I could not even read them. They were written in some kind of code. The pages were filled with tiny, closely packed letters that made no sense, although I could occasionally make out a date. It was all very mysterious. I could tell that the writing was in my aunt's hand, but I wondered what in the world she would have to write that she felt best put in code, and why would these notebooks be kept hidden in a secret drawer along with a gun and an old key? All this was very strange.

When Greg came that evening I showed him the notebooks. He looked at them for a long time, a frown on his face. He turned the pages slowly, examining the curious lettering. His gray-green eyes had a curious expression in them, and one corner of his mouth was turned down.

"Can you read any of it?" I asked.

"Not a word," he replied.

"I can't imagine what they might contain, what Aunt Lucille possibly could have written that she would have wanted to put in code. Perhaps the notebooks contain medicinal recipes, something to do with herbs."

"Do you mind if I take them with me?" Greg asked. "I know a little about codes. Perhaps I could decipher them for you."

"I would appreciate that," I replied. "Perhaps they will tell me something more about my aunt."

"Undoubtedly," Greg said, his voice low. For a moment I had the strange impression that he had been able to read the notes and had discovered something unpleasant that he wanted to keep from me. I looked at his face closely. There were lines of worry about his eyes, and his jaw was thrust out. He seemed to be lost in thought.

"Is anything wrong, Greg?" I asked.

He looked up, still frowning. Then he seemed to relax, heaving a sigh.

"Not really," he said, trying to smile. "I had some bad news today and it's disturbed me a little. My brother in Liverpool is having some business trouble and I am going to have to go and help him out for a few days."

"I didn't know you had a brother, Greg. You've never mentioned him to me."

"Haven't I? Wayne is the only family I have left. He's older than I, has a small printing press in Liverpool. He's the salt of the earth, good, steady —too good. He's about to lose his printing press. I think maybe I can look over the books and talk to the creditors and straighten things out. He really knows nothing about the business, keeps in the back of the shop with the ink and the glue and presses and lets others manage all the actual business transactions. His assistant has embezzled some money and run away, leaving Wayne in a bad fix."

"I'm so sorry to hear that, Greg. How long will you be gone?"

"About a week. Roderick's ball is on the fifth of April. I will get back that afternoon, in plenty of time for the great occasion. Stephenson is going to double up and take over my classes, so the school doesn't mind letting me go."

Greg stood up, gathering up the notebooks from the table. "I will take these along. Maybe I'll have some time to work on them. Take care of yourself while I'm gone, Angela."

"I will, Greg. You do the same."

He left and I spent a long time thinking about what had happened. I had not told Greg about the gun and the key, and I took them out now and examined them again. I looked at the gun and wondered if my aunt had ever used it. It was a pretty thing, so small and well made, but it could be deadly, too. I held the key in my hand, wondering what it unlocked. The gun, the key, the notebooks in the secret drawer—all of them imposed a mystery, and it baffled me. I felt that if I ever found the lock that this key fit I would also find the solution to the mystery of it all.

8

I waited nervously for Greg to come, feeling strange in all my new finery. I stood in the parlor where the last rays of tangerine sunlight were dying on the old ivory walls. I was afraid to sit down lest I rumple the dress, for I wanted to be flawless when Greg arrived. I had not heard from him, and as the clock ticked on in the silence of the room and the sunlight was replaced by long blue shadows, I paced restlessly, and foolishly, for he was to arrive at seven thirty and it was just shortly after seven now.

Nan had spent over an hour over my hair, arranging the light brown waves skillfully on top of my head, with three long ringlets dangling down to touch my naked shoulder. The dress was a thing of beauty, the bodice of red satin cut low, very tight at the waist, adorned with amethyst ribbons, the skirt great swirls of red satin overlaid with shimmering folds of amethyst. I had never worn such a dress, and it gave me a strange feeling of power. I felt like a different person, older, wiser and ready to handle any situation with skill. I was no longer a humble seamstress who had accidentally become the owner of a house in the country. I was a great lady to whom anything might happen.

Yet, at the same time, I was apprehensive. I was in masquerade. I looked at the beautiful woman in the full length mirror, and I still saw the former seamstress, nervously clutching her hands in fear that her escort would not arrive on time.

I was very excited about going to Phoenix Hall. The whole county was talking about the ball, about the lavish preparations that had been made, about the gentry who would be there, about the special food and wine ordered all the way from London, about the musicians Mellory had hired to play for his guests. Some said that Roderick Mellory had prepared Phoenix Hall for his bride and would chose her from all the well brought up young maidens who would attend the ball. Others said that this was his way of flaunting his wealth and power in the faces of those who would not attend, the villagers of Lockwood, who would not even be allowed to stand out in the gardens and watch the grand affair through the windows. Nan had related all this gossip to me, adding and embellishing with her own opinions. There had been no affair like this in Lockwood since Mellory's father had given his memorable balls, many years ago.

When Greg finally arrived, I was a little alarmed at his appearance. He looked very tired, and I could understand this. He had just returned from a long, exhausting trip. But there was something else about his face that I could not quite fathom. There were furrows between his brows and tired lines about the corners of the eyes, and the eyes themselves looked cloudy and disturbed, as though they had seen something distressing. There was a small droop at the corner of his mouth. He seemed preoccupied with something.

He stood looking at me for a long time, but it was almost as though he were not seeing me. Although his eyes were on me, they seemed to be seeing something else entirely.

"You look ravishing," he said. "The dress is lovely."

"Thank you, Greg. You look tired."

"It was a long journey, a hard one."

"Did everything go well?"

"As well as could be expected," he said evasively.

"Is there anything I can do?" I asked.

He looked away from me, creasing his brows as though he was making a grave decision. He wore his handsome evening clothes casually, as though he was accustomed to them. The silky black jacket fit tightly about his shoulders, the wide black satin lapels turned back to reveal a gleaming white shirtfront and a dark maroon waistband. He wore a white tie and the lining of his swirling evening cape was of heavy white satin. Greg would look at home at Whitehall, I thought. He might be a young lord or a member of Parliament. It was hard to believe, seeing him like this, that he was merely a country schoolteacher.

He looked into my eyes, his own suddenly very serious.

"You asked if there was anything you could do," he said. "There may be something, Angela. You can believe in me. You can have faith in me. I need that just now. There is—" He paused for a moment, trying to find the right words. "Something big has come up, something I can't explain just now. It's what I've been looking for all my life. It would mean leaving this place, leaving the school. It would mean the fulfillment of all my dreams. And I would like for you to be a part of it, Angela."

"Greg, you're—you're talking in riddles. I don't know exactly what you are trying to say."

He smiled. It was a feeble smile. Then he shook his head slowly and seemed to relax.

"I know. It wasn't fair of me to spring it like that and not give you any of the details. I can't tell you what it's all about yet. All I need to know is that you're behind me."

"Of course I am, Greg. You should know that."

"It will make all the difference," he said.

I studied him for a moment, wondering what all this could be about. The worried look was gone from his face, and in its place was a look of excitement and anticipation. He looked like a schoolboy who had just been given a prolonged holiday and had months of freedom ahead. I did not know how to take this sudden change. Something important had happened. I knew that he would tell me about it when the time came and until then I could only do as he asked, have faith in him.

He put both his hands on my shoulders and looked into my eyes. He was smiling now and those light gray eyes with their specks of green held an emotion that I understood immediately and was afraid of. I did not want us to stop being friends. I valued the easy, relaxed companionship we shared, and I was not ready to exchange it for something new. He was very dear to me as a friend, but it would take time to learn if I could feel anything more than this present warmth and admiration.

"I'm very happy, Angela," he said.

"I am glad, Greg."

"I want you to be happy, too. I want you to share in my happiness."

"I—I don't know," I replied quietly.

"Have patience with me," he said. "I don't want to tell you about all this until I am certain of everything. When I present my plan it is going to be perfect, with no loose ends. In a few days, maybe, I will know for sure. You'll be patient, Angela?"

I nodded. He smiled again, taking my arm. My skirts rustled as I walked outside with him. It was dark now, but in the moonlight I could see his face and the flashing white lining of his cape as he helped me into the carriage. He picked up the reins in one hand and stretched his other arm about my shoulder, pulling me close beside him. We drove to Phoenix Hall slowly, and I felt a sadness I could not comprehend. Something was lost, and I grieved for it, but I didn't know yet just what it was I was grieving for.

9

*S*ensation piled upon sensation, too fast, too bright, too beautiful for me to catch them all. We walked down the stairs into the ballroom to the lively strains of music, and I heard laughter and voices and could see a hundred faces turned up to watch us. A buzz went through the crowd, and I heard people talking about us and asking who I was. I leaned on Greg's arm for support, very nervous at this close inspection.

I saw men young and old in their handsome suits and uniforms, women in spectacular gowns of every color, whirling brilliantly on the floor. Three huge chandeliers dripped from the gold leaf ceiling, and the reflections of a thousand candles made the crystal pendants glitter with all the colors of the rainbow.

"You're trembling," Greg whispered, grinning.

"I can't help it."

"Hold your head up, Angela. You are by far the loveliest woman here tonight."

"Don't say silly things. I feel light-headed as it is."

My head seemed to whirl in fast spins. There was too much dazzle and too much color. I wanted to turn and run. I did not belong here. Prim, reserved Miss Angela Todd had no place in a glittering ballroom, I told myself, and yet I felt a certain pride at being with a man as handsome as Greg. This whole evening was like a schoolgirl's dream come true, and I was as nervous as any schoolgirl could have been.

"Who is that woman with Greg Ingram?" I heard a woman ask.

"I've never seen her," another replied, "but I wonder where she got that gown. Have you ever seen anything so lovely?"

"From Paris, more than likely. She's probably someone from London, a former flame of Roderick's."

"With Greg Ingram? It's hardly likely, my dear."

"This place is swarming with Roderick's former flames. They say that Lady Miriam Alton is even coming."

"She wouldn't *dare.*"

"Miriam would do anything."

I wondered who the controversial Lady Miriam was and what connection she had with Roderick Mellory. I did not doubt that it was a scandalous one. All these people seemed strange creatures to me, their lives so far removed from my own that I could only look at them in awe, as one would peer at bizarre and beautiful animals in a zoo.

We moved on. I saw an ancient soldier with silver gray hair, golden braid draped all over the shoulders of his royal blue jacket. He was talking to a dark eyed woman whose jet black gown was resplendent with a thousand glittering jet beads. Her lined cheeks had too much rouge on them, her eyelids were heavily coated with mauve shadow and her hair was a blazing artificial red. She peered at us through a lorgnette as we passed, and the soldier stroked a silver moustache and eyed me with appreciation.

"The affluent ones," Greg commented. "Don't let them intimidate you, Angela. That old woman might look like a dragon, but she would give every diamond she has for your complexion."

"Who is Lady Miriam Alton?" I asked.

"A stunning brunette of thirty-five, something of a scandal to the English peerage. She has an ancient husband, an ancient estate, and some very modern ideas."

"Meaning?"

Greg smiled at my curiosity. "Meaning that she often makes the headlines in the tabloids and scandal sheets."

"Oh, one of those creatures," I said disapprovingly.

"Lady Miriam isn't so bad," Greg replied, plainly amused by my comment. "She tends to live with a bit more dash and color than most of the nobility. A moldering estate and a moldering husband aren't quite enough to satisfy her appetite for life."

"You admire her?"

"I've never met her, just heard about her."

I wondered why I should be so curious about Lady Miriam Alton. I did not know why I should feel such sudden resentment for a woman I had never laid eyes on.

"Everyone should live with dash and color," Greg said.

"Should they?"

"Life is more than being a seamstress or a schoolteacher. A man has to reach out and grab life. A man has to force it into the shape desired. Or else remain a schoolteacher the rest of his life."

"Would that be such a bad life, Greg?" I asked.

He did not reply. There was no need to. Greg was a complex person. He was very dissatisfied, just how dissatisfied I was only beginning to see now. He looked so very much a part of this crowd. He was as elegant, as handsome as any man present. He moved with confidence, as one who belonged, and yet he did not belong any more than I did. I could see how difficult that must be for him.

"Shall we dance, Angela?" he said, bowing slightly.

The music swirled dramatically as Greg took me into his arms. We were all at once a moving, spinning part of a multicolored kaleidoscope. I saw the sparkle of diamonds and emeralds, the flashing wings of colored satin skirts, the grace and excitement of a world I had never known. I closed my eyes, and the lights were still there. I felt the strong support of Greg's arm, felt his body guiding mine. The music swelled and shattered and swelled again, great waves of music engulfing us and moving us. I was dizzy. My cheeks flushed with excitement.

For a few moments I did belong. I was a part. Phoenix Hall and the beautiful people were as natural for me as for Lady Miriam or for anyone else. It was a glorious, heady feeling, but it disappeared as soon as the music stopped. I was brought back to reality with an abrupt halt. I opened my eyes to see strangers, people I could never know.

I was not disappointed. I had Dower House. I had more than I had ever had before.

"You look lovely with your cheeks flushed," Greg said. "You should always have that flush of excitement. You should always wear lovely gowns and dance with your eyes closed."

I wished I could agree with him, but I knew that lovely gowns, glittering ballrooms would always be alien to me, and I was not sorry. Greg took my hand and led me standing beside a slender white column as he went for champagne.

I peered around a bank of lacy green fern at a group of young women, exquisite, radiant creatures in pale satin gowns, chattering and laughing. They were like gorgeous butterflies. I wondered if these were some of the prospective brides Nan had spoken of. Would Roderick Mellory choose one of them to be mistress of Phoenix Hall?

I realized then what I had been aware of all evening: I was anxiously awaiting sight of that man. I had been looking for him ever since we had arrived, but I had refused to acknowledge it to myself. I wanted to see Roderick Mellory again. I hated him. I loathed everything he stood for, and yet the mere expectation of seeing him caused my pulse to race. Can hatred do that to a person? I wondered.

He was my enemy, and yet I had come to enemy ground of my own choice and with every expectation of seeing him and speaking to him again. I told myself that I had come for Laurel's sake, to make her happy, and because Greg wanted me to accompany him, but I knew now that I had come because of Roderick Mellory. I was spoiling for a fight.

As I stood by the column two old people wandered by. The man was bent over and walked with an ivory-handled cane. The woman had brownish, papery skin and watery blue eyes. Her silver hair was piled in splendid waves on top of her head, and her scarlet gown was sprinkled with rhinestones. The gown hung loosely on her old body.

"Phoenix Hall has never been so resplendent," the man said as he went hobbling past. "Not even in its prime. I remember the days when—"

"Roderick Mellory must have spent a fortune, several fortunes," the woman replied, cutting short her companion's remarks. "Where did he manage to get the money for all these repairs?"

"He's a resourceful young man."

"Resourceful? Perhaps, but hardly honest. No honest man makes the kind of money Roderick Mellory has made in the last few years. I would give a lot to know just *how* he made the money to refurbish Phoenix Hall."

"They say he's a very keen businessman."

"They say a lot of things about him," the woman snapped. "If half of the things they say are true—"

They passed on, and I found myself wondering the same thing the old woman had wondered about. How did Roderick Mellory make the money to begin such costly repairs on the estate? I supposed there must be ways of making a fortune, particularly if one had some money to begin with, but it did seem curious. I did not doubt that many of the business transactions Roderick Mellory engaged in were dishonest.

I saw Greg approaching from across the room. As I watched, one of the servants tapped him on the shoulder and said something into his ear. Greg asked the man a question, and when the servant replied I thought I saw a curious expression pass over Greg's face. What was it? Fear? Anger? Alarm? The servant left, and Greg stood there for a moment, his brow pressed into a deep frown. Splendidly dressed people moved past him, some of them speaking to him. Greg did not reply. After a while he looked up, saw me waiting and hurried over. He brought a glass of champagne.

"Sorry," he said, smiling. He handed me the champagne.

"Is anything wrong?" I asked.

"Why do you ask that?"

"You look so—crestfallen. Worried."

He grinned. "Nonsense," he replied.

"What did that servant want?" I asked. "The one who spoke to you?"

He looked up sharply. "You saw?"

"Yes. It—it looked as though he had some kind of bad news."

Greg looked into my eyes. His own were very hard, and his lips were pressed tightly together. Who is this man? I wondered. I don't know him. He had been so strange earlier this evening at the cottage, and now he was a complete stranger.

"What is it, Greg?" I asked, my voice very firm.

"I'm sorry," he said, relaxing into his old self. He took my hand in his and squeezed it. "I didn't want to spoil your evening, Angela. This is a big night for you. I wanted it to be perfect. Now this —oh, damn. I may as well tell you. One of the boys at school has taken ill, seriously ill. The doctor has no idea what it is. The lad's been sniffling for days. He is one of the boarders and his parents can't be reached—there's nothing I can do, but I really should be there."

"Of course you should," I said.

"But, dammit—"

"You would worry all evening, Greg. Go to him."

"What about you? The ball—"

"You can take me home first."

Laurel Mellory came over to us then, seeming to float like a butterfly in her blue and silver gown, the skirts billowing like wings. Her silvery blonde hair was stacked in glossy waves on top of her head, caught up with blue velvet ribbons, and three long curls dangled over her naked shoulder. Her face was animated. Her dark blue eyes were full of excitement. Laurel took my hand and smiled, very pleased to see me.

"Oh, Angela. It's so nice. These people terrify me. They're all so grand! Isn't it exciting! You must stay by me to give me support. I have been looking all over for you. I didn't see you come in. I was afraid that you wouldn't come—" Her voice bubbled with enthusiasm, and her young face was almost beautiful.

"I am afraid I must leave, Laurel," I said quietly, and then I explained what had happened. Greg added a few words, making his apologies in a sober voice. The sparkle went out of Laurel's face, and she lowered her lids in disappointment.

"No," she said. "You mustn't go—Greg, of course, you must, but let Angela stay. The ball has hardly begun. We have such magnificent food, and I so wanted you to be here, Angela—"

"I'm sorry, Laurel—"

"No, you must stay," she said, like the child she

actually was. "You can have one of the carriages to go home in. I'll have Clark drive you back to Dower House. Yes, yes, that's what we'll do."

Greg looked at me with questioning eyes. I nodded my head.

"Very well," he said. "Come with me to get my cloak, Angela."

We left Laurel and went back up the stairs to the grand hall. I waited as Greg claimed his cloak. I did not want to stay. The grandness of the people, the glamor of the mansion, the beauty of the music had already put me in a pensive, depressed mood. I wanted to be alone in my simple little parlor. I wanted to sit and sew and be plain Angela Todd. I did not want to masquerade as something I wasn't.

"I feel rotten, leaving you like this," Greg said, wrapping his rich swirls of cloak about his shoulders.

"It couldn't be helped," I replied.

"No—no, I suppose it couldn't," he answered, his voice hard. I was surprised at the tone. "Damn the boy, anyway," he said. "I don't want to leave you like this. I wanted tonight to be our night, Angela. There is so much I want for us."

He was very intense. Two small spots of color glowed on his fine cheekbones, and his gray eyes were piercing. I reached up and pushed a lock of hair from his forehead, and he caught my fingers, gripping them tightly in his hand. I winced.

"Greg—"

"There is so much I want for you."

"Please—" He was hurting me.

He released me. We walked down the hall and he found a servant and requested that his carriage be sent around front. We walked outside, onto the porch with the curving marble stairs. It was cool, with small zephyrs of wind rustling the ivy on the walls. The sky was a cold, hard black, a few frosty stars glittering like bits of ice. The drive curled in front of us, one solitary light casting a silver glow on the crushed shell. I stood at the railing, my palms resting on the cool marble. Greg stood behind me. I could feel his body near mine, and I could smell the leathery, male smell of him.

I was uneasy. I did not know why. The ball and all its color was behind us, all the noise and gaiety shut off behind the heavy oak doors. I was trembling, but I attributed that to the breeze on my uncovered shoulders. I was afraid of what Greg might say. I did not want him to say anything. I wanted the carriage to come and this moment to end.

He was a fine man. He was a very dear friend. He had been wonderful to me ever since I had come to Dower House. He was intelligent, handsome, poised, the kind of man any woman would be fortunate to have, but I did not want him to stop being my friend. I did not want him to become anything more, not just yet. I did not know him, not really, and I did not know myself well enough to sort out the curious emotions I felt.

"You're shivering," he said, putting his hands on my shoulders.

I shrugged, trying to compose myself.

"It's nothing," I said. "The carriage will be here in a moment."

"You'll catch cold," he replied, his voice very gentle, "and it would be my fault. I wouldn't want anything bad to come to you because of me. Here—" He took off his cloak and wrapped it around me, smoothing it over my arms and shoulders.

"Better now?" he asked, adjusting the heavy satin folds.

I cast about in my mind to find something to say, anything to relieve the tension I felt.

"Greg—the—the notebooks, Aunt Lucille's notebooks, have you been able to do anything with them? You said you might be able to decipher the code. Have you worked on it?"

"I haven't had time," he replied.

"I'm so curious about them. I am eager to see what they contain. Do you think you'll be able to get to them soon?"

"I don't know."

"It was so strange, their being locked in that secret drawer, and the gun and the key." I had not meant to say this. Greg didn't know of them and I was irritated with myself for having let it slip out.

"The gun? The key?"

"There was a gun in the drawer, a fancy little gun, and a key. I've no idea what the key unlocks."

"Why didn't you tell me about them?"

"I—I don't know. I didn't think it important."

He did not reply. The silence hung heavy. There was the muted sound of the music, closed off, a faint suggestion of music that only made the silence more uncomfortable. I kept wishing I would hear the sound of hoof beats and the crunch of wheels on the drive.

"Aunt Lucille was a rather enigmatic figure," I said. "I wish I had known her, really known her. What a strange old woman she must have been with her herbs and poisons and secret drawers and revolvers and keys. You really must decipher those notebooks. Or, better yet, if you don't have time, I can send them to London. There must be someone who can decipher them, perhaps that old man who works in the museum. I used to talk about Egypt to him everytime I went, and he seemed to know a lot about all the scripts and things—"

I was babbling nervously, and Greg had not said a word. It was quite clear, I had irritated him. He did not want to talk about notebooks and old men who worked in museums. I turned around to face him. I could barely see his face. In the darkness it was a large, pale oval with the jaw thrust out angrily. His eyes were hard and did not conceal his irritation.

"Would you like me to take the notebooks back?" I asked. "I don't want to trouble you, and I'm sure someone in London—"

"Why are you so curious about the notebooks?" Greg said. His voice was level, low pitched.

"Isn't curiosity natural?" I replied.

"Forget them, Angela," he said. "Forget about sending them away. I will get to them one of these days. Soon. Damn, I wish that groom would hurry with the carriage! I'm worried about the boy."

"I know, Greg," I replied, trying to sound comforting.

He *was* worried, and it was admirable in him. Greg was devoted to those boys he taught, and he was willing to give up his own pleasure in order to be at the bedside of one of them, even when his presence could do no real good. That was admirable too. He had been acting strangely tonight, but then he had just returned from a long and arduous journey to Liverpool. He said that his brother's business affairs were in a terrible tangle, and he had had to untangle them. That could not have been pleasant. He had arrived in Lockwood only in time to bathe and change into his formal attire so that he could take me to this ball.

I should appreciate all that, I told myself, and I should not grow all tense and nervous because I'm afraid he is going to declare himself. I should be proud and happy that a man like Greg Ingram is even interested in me. Greg was interested; he had made that clear this evening at Dower House. I should have been ecstatic at my good fortune, but something darker, stronger held me back from responding to Greg. I did not know yet what it was, but I knew it wasn't in Greg's power to unleash that force.

"I suppose I made a fool of myself at Dower House this evening," he remarked crisply. "Talking like that, telling you my plans, asking you to share them with me."

"Don't talk like that, Greg."

"I asked a foolish question. I told you foolish things."

"No, Greg," I said quietly. "It was not foolish."

"I wanted to share with someone, with you."

"I understand. Your plan—whatever it is, whatever you are going to do that will be so important —I understand. I want to share your excitement about it. You deserve the best, Greg."

"Do I?"

"Of course."

"The best is you," he said, his voice flat.

"Greg—"

"You feel nothing?"

"I—of course I do."

"You don't show it."

"Greg—"

"I've tried to make myself clear, my feelings—"

"You are the best friend I have, Greg."

"Friend? Yes. I have your friendship."

"Isn't that enough?" I asked. I knew the moment the words left my lips that they were the wrong words.

He laughed quietly. It was a bitter laugh.

"Enough?" he said. "What is enough? You work hard all your life, and you get respect. You toil, you give up, you sacrifice so that you can make something of yourself, and you end up in a country school. You have the respect and admiration of the people, oh yes, and you have the condescending patronage of gentry like the Mellorys, but that's all you have. Tell me, is that enough?"

"For many people it would be," I replied.

"But I am different. I want more than left-overs."

"You are being unfair to yourself, Greg."

"Am I? I want more than respect. I want more than admiration. I want fine things. I want to be able to hold my head high. I want to be powerful. I want to be able to stand beside men like Roderick Mellory and feel equal, equal in every way."

I made no reply. There were no words I could say that would help. I did not know what I could do to make him see how wrong he was. How could I show him that he was twice the man that Roderick Mellory was? How could I let him know that he was worth more, far more? There was only one way, and I could not bring myself to play false. I could not pretend to feel something that I did not feel.

"You will have all the things you want," I finally said. "You must give yourself time."

"Time? There isn't much time, Angela."

He stood back. I could see the expression on his face, and it hurt me. It hurt me to think that I was partly responsible for that expression. I laid my hand gently on his cheek. After a moment he relaxed. He heaved his chest and sighed heavily. It was as if all the energy was suddenly drained out of him.

"Forgive me," he said in his natural voice. "I don't know what brought on this outburst. It was uncalled for."

"You are exhausted. The long trip, this boy's sudden illness—"

"I suppose that's it. You will forgive me?"

"You don't even need to ask that."

I heard the carriage coming up the drive. I thought it was one of the loveliest sounds I had ever heard. It circled in front of the porch and stopped. The groom began to climb down. In the semidarkness I saw the satiny sheen of the horse's coat.

Greg took both my hands in his. He pressed them tightly.

"I am sorry to leave you like this," he said. "You understand?"

"You know I do. Be careful. And let me know about the child."

"I will, Angela. Enjoy the rest of the ball."

He held my hands a minute longer and then left, without saying another word. It was only after he had climbed into the carriage and was driving away that I realized I was still wearing his cloak. It was much too large for me, the heavy satin folds completely engulfing my body, but I stood there holding it tightly about me. I did not want to go inside just yet. The cloak smelled strongly of his pungent, masculine scent. I stroked the black satin lapels, thinking about the strange, misplaced man to whom the garment belonged.

10

The house was filled with sound. The music rose and swelled in bright waves and against this there was the sound of people laughing and talking. I left Greg's cloak with an attendant and stood in the hall for a moment. I did not feel like joining Laurel just yet. I had experienced too many emotions, too quickly, and I had not had time to pull myself together. There was a large mirror in a heavily ornate frame hanging on the wall across from me, and I caught sight of myself.

My eyes seemed very large and dark, with shadows under them, and the wind had disarrayed the neat coiffure Nan had worked so hard on. It had stung bright spots of color on my cheeks. I stared at myself. The red satin gown did not seem appropriate with the messed hair and the dark eyes. I wondered what I was doing here in this grand house, hearing the bright music and all the gaily chattering voices. I was like a plain pebble in a box of diamonds, and I did not belong. I wanted to run away, to be alone so that I could sort out my emotions, but my loyalty to Laurel made me stay.

I could not face the people just yet. I walked down the hall and found a door ajar. I opened it and stepped into a small sitting room. It was all in darkness, but a shaft of moonlight fell through the parted drapes, making a shimmering bar of silver in which tiny motes whirled. I stepped into the room, pulling the door closed behind me. I could see a dark blue couch and the outlines of an ivory-topped table, touched by the moonlight, but the rest of the room was a nest of shadows.

I stood very quietly, breathing unevenly, holding my hand against my heart. I had not known just how unnerved I had been after the scene with Greg. I felt that I had been unjust with him, and I knew that I had hurt him. Greg was a fine person, truly a gentle man, and it was not right that he should have to suffer because of me. It was a shame that he could not see what a marvelous thing he was doing in Lockwood, that he should be dissatisfied with his job and his position. There was no one in all the county who was more respected than Greg Ingram. That in itself was much more than most men attained.

I heard voices outside the room, and there was a crack of light near the floor across the room. It was another door, and it must lead directly into the grand foyer and ballroom. I stepped across the room and tried to open the door. It was locked, but I felt the key still in place. When I had unlocked the door I pulled it open slowly, just enough to see out.

People were passing through the foyer, and beyond I could see people dancing in the ballroom,

turning in whirls of color beneath the glittering
chandeliers. I stood there for a long while, holding the door open but standing back in the darkness so that no one could see me. I saw Laurel
talking to a young man with pink cheeks and
short gold hair. He wore a uniform, and a sword
dangled from its loose scabard. Laurel talked
with animation, making pretty gestures with her
hands, but she kept glancing over her shoulders,
and I knew that she was looking for me.

Then I took a deep breath, gasping aloud in the
darkened room. Roderick Mellory was walking
down the foyer, coming near and nearer the
room where I stood. By his side, clinging to his
arm, was one of the grandest women I had ever
seen. Her scarlet lips were parted in a half smile,
and her chin was held at an arrogant angle. Her
eyes were hard, the color of dark blue ink, and
they were looking up at Roderick Mellory with
cold, calculating possession. I knew instantly that
this was Lady Miriam Alton, and I knew as
quickly that she intended to be the new Mistress
of Phoenix Hall.

My heart was pounding, but I could not force
myself to step back and pull the door shut. They
sauntered nearer, speaking in quiet voices, and I
watched with fascination.

Roderick Mellory wore a dark black suit, the
pants very tight, clinging to his legs. The jacket
was loose, with dark satin lapels and cuffs, and
long tails that fell away in back. He wore it over a
vest of sky blue satin, stitched with silver designs.
He wore the formal attire casually, as though they
might be work clothes, and his hair was un-
combed, spilling in lustrous blue black waves
over his head. One brow was arched like a dark

wing, and the hooded lids were half closed, veiling the dark eyes. He held his head to one side, listening to what Lady Miriam said, with his lips curled in a smile of cynical amusement. I thought of a dark panther, moving arrogantly with rippling muscles.

If Roderick Mellory reminded me of a panther, Lady Miriam Alton made me think of a serpent, cold, glittering and fascinating, but deadly. She wore a gown of emerald satin, heavily embroidered with jet, and the skirt was trimmed with great pelts of sable. Diamonds flashed on her wrists and fingers like chunks of frozen fire, dazzling in their beauty. The bodice of her gown was cut indecently low, trimmed with the same rich sable as was the skirt. Long, curling plumes of black and green were fastened on her sleek black hair with a diamond clip. She was incredibly glamorous, a creature that legends were formed around, and I hated every inch of her lovely body.

"Phoenix Hall should always abound with life like this," she said. Her voice was throaty, husky, as glamorous as the rest of her. "Things like this ball should happen every week, people, music, sin."

"You think so?" Roderick Mellory said.

"Darling, it's such a *big* place. It needs life, much life, action. It could so easily become a musty old hall, like my husband's. That would be a shame, no—a crime. A terrible crime. You wouldn't commit a crime, Roderick, would you?"

They stopped a few feet from the door. I trembled with fear that he would turn around and see me, but his back was to me, and Lady Miriam was much too engrossed to notice anything but the man before her.

"What do you think?" he asked.

Lady Miriam held her head back, looking into his eyes. A smile began to curl on her sensual scarlet lips, and she emitted a husky laugh. It was a fascinating sound, and evil. She touched his cheek with her fingertips. They stroked his leathery skin.

"Oh, yes," she said, her voice barely a whisper, "I think you are capable of committing a crime—any crime—to get what you want."

"Like adultery, my dear?" he asked.

"It's a thought," she replied.

"You're thoroughly corrupt," he told her, chuckling.

"Darling, aren't we *both?*"

"I imagine you're right."

"We would make a marvelous pair. Think of it —you and I in this wonderful place, think of the parties, the excitement."

"I am thinking of Lord Peter Alton," he replied.

"Pooh! Peter would divorce me in a minute. He would be glad to have me out of his hair. Poor dear, I've tormented him so long. It's such a bore, tormenting an old man. It's time for *me* to be tormented, and I am sure you would torment any woman—"

They moved away, Lady Miriam's skirts rustling stiffly. I felt blood rushing to my cheeks, and I tried to still the anger that possessed me. It would serve Roderick Mellory right to have such a woman, I told myself. It would be poetic justice for them to destroy one another. It did not concern me in the least. And yet my cheeks still burned and my heart pounded in my breast like something trapped and fighting to get out.

Why? I did not know, or I told myself that. Every time I was near this man I felt the same excitement, and I called it hatred. I hated him, how I hated him. He was arrogant, cruel, a dark, cynical devil who wanted to take Dower House away from me, and I was determined to block him every way I knew how. Yes, it was hatred, only hatred that made me feel this way.

I told myself that, but I knew I was lying to myself.

I turned back into the darkened room, closing the door. I stood there, leaning against the door. My eyes were closed, and the music and the ball seemed very far away. I felt weak, depleted of energy. Then I heard something rustle in the room, and there was the sound of heavy breathing. I gave a little cry, suddenly terrified.

There was a loud scrape as a match was struck, then a ball of light as the match was held over a lamp wick. Warm golden-orange light spread slowly into the room, driving the shadows away. I stood panting against the door, seeing first a smiling mouth, then two large, sad eyes, and finally, when the light was steady, I saw the young man in the wheelchair. He was wearing a suit like his brother's and a rich red and brown plaid blanket covered his injured legs.

"I did not mean to frighten you," he said.

"Paul—"

I was terribly embarrassed. I felt that I had been caught doing something wrong. He stared up at me with those large eyes, and I turned my face away, not wanting him to see what was there. He set the lamp on the desk. I heard the wheels creaking as he moved himself out of the corner.

"I started to call out when you first came into

the room but I could see that you were upset. I didn't want to alarm you."

"You've been there all this time? Watching me?"

"It was rude," Paul Mellory said. "I should have spoken."

"I—I don't know what to say. I feel like a fool."

"You mustn't say anything, Angela. It is for me to apologize. I had no business sitting here, watching you."

"But—why aren't you with the others?" I asked.

Once again, as with Greg, I knew that I had said the wrong thing, but I could not take back the words. It was obvious why he wasn't with all the others, as obvious as the bright plaid blanket drawn over his broken legs. He was stoic, he tried not to show his emotions, but I knew what torture it must be to see people laughing and dancing, moving in bright patterns across the ballroom while he was confined to a wheelchair. That it was his own home must make it even harder to bear. I knew why he had come here, away from the noise and excitement. He had come here in order to suffer in silence, alone.

"Please forgive me," I said.

A thin smile played on his lips, twisting them down at the corners. I could see the pain in his eyes. My question had been cruel, unintentionally, yet nevertheless cruel. Paul Mellory composed himself, his face moving into the defiant mask he wore with other people.

"Nonsense. You know I am not sensitive," he lied. "That would be insane in my position. Sensitive people only get hurt." He tried very hard to sound like his brother, but his voice wavered.

"Would you like me to leave?" I asked quietly.

"Oh, no. Stay and talk to me. You are human,

unlike those chattering magpies out there. Have you ever seen such a group? The cream of the cream, all gathered together to eat our food and drink our champagne and then go home and criticize the Mellorys. How I loathe them."

I hated to see him so bitter, but there was nothing I could say.

"You look very beautiful tonight," he remarked. "The dress is lovely and just right. No diamonds, no flowers, just your youth. That's fitting and proper. What did you think of Lady Miriam?"

"You saw me watching?"

"I couldn't help but see."

"She is—very lovely."

"Yes, she is that," Paul Mellory said.

"Your—your brother seemed quite taken with her," I said.

"Oh, Lady Miriam amuses him. All this amuses him. He wanted to show off in front of all the county, and he wanted to do it in style. They will talk about this ball for months. They will talk about the expense he went to. They will call it ostentatious, but they will talk. That is what my brother wants."

"That seems a rather hollow reason for giving a ball." I remarked.

"Not really. If Phoenix Hall is to be what it was before, if it is to have the same prestige, it must be grand, there must be grand balls to impress the people. There must be music and lights and extravagance. Rod has been very extravagant. We may eat bread and soup for a month now, but he had made his point."

"That seems pretentious," I said.

"Isn't all life a pretense?"

"Not for everyone," I replied, primly.

"You're right. Not for everyone. Not for you. You are sincere. You don't need to pretend. But you are fortunate. You have something rare, an independent heart, and it will carry you through most anything, but others are not so lucky. They need something to support them, some pretense. Rod needs to believe that Phoenix Hall is what it can never be again, a power in the county, a grand estate. Times have changed, and they're changing still. The days of grand estates are vanishing, but my brother needs the illusion."

"That is sad," I said quietly.

"Not necessarily. Illusions can be very satisfying when one works hard to maintain them. They can give a purpose to life, as they have done for Rod."

He looked up at me with those dark brown eyes. His long lashes curled about them, the color of soot, and there were mauve shadows on his lids. I felt great compassion for this brave, doomed boy. I wondered what illusion he clung to.

"You brother has done a magnificent job with Phoenix Hall," I said. "I think it is lovely."

"Yes, he's done a good job. He works hard, drives himself and everyone around him. He's a fighter. Now that Phoenix Hall is in shape, he will fight even harder for Dower House."

"Really?"

"You won't give in?"

"I've already made that clear."

"I wish you would. I wish you'd leave Dower House. My brother would be very generous. You could go back to London, open your own dress shop. I would like to know you were safe."

"Safe?"

"I worry about you, Angela. All alone in that place."

"I'm quite safe. I have Nan, and Peter."

"I worry just the same—"

"Why?" I asked, suddenly alert.

"The lights—" He paused, looked at my face and became silent.

"What lights, Paul?" I already knew, but I must hear his words.

"The lights in the deserted granite quarries behind Dower House," Paul said slowly. "I—I don't mean to alarm you." He hesitated again.

"Please go on, Paul."

"Two nights ago I was sitting in the garden, the far one nearest Dower House. I had been reading. Roderick had gone away on business, and Laurel was resting. She had a headache. I didn't feel like wheeling myself back to the house just then, so I sat there, watching the sun go down. I must have fallen asleep, because when I woke up the moon was already high, and I was cold. It was then that I saw the lights."

"In the quarry?"

"Yes. Far away, bobbing up and down, like someone was climbing over the rocks with a hodded lantern."

"Are you sure that you didn't imagine it?"

"I am positive. Something had awakened me, some noise. It could have been a shout—a sound would carry a long way among these rocks. I listened but there was no other sound. In a moment the lights disappeared."

"There was more than one?"

"Two, at least. Possibly three. They were just pinpoints of light, from the distance."

"I have seen the lights, too," I said. "I am sure

there must be a perfectly logical explanation for them."

"You know that the highwaymen struck again two nights ago?"

"No," I said, my voice very low. "I didn't know."

"They did. On the coastal road, about ten miles from here. There was a coach delivering goods from London, and gold sovereigns. They were using the old road and traveling at night to divert suspicion. That coach had to come through, and only a handful of people knew what it was carrying. The highwaymen struck around eight o'clock."

"How did they know?" I asked, suddenly breathless.

"That is the major question. The officials have pinpointed them to the area around here. Someone—someone big in local affairs must be involved in these attacks. Their hideout is definitely in this area, and the local constable feels that it is somewhere in the quarries."

"Haven't they searched them?"

"Several times. But the quarries are vast. There's a whole network of caves and tunnels. The one behind Dower House is merely one of a series. It connects with others, larger. It was just a rumor before, but now it's almost a certainty. This is the closest the highwaymen have ever struck to Lockwood, and after they hit, half the men in the county were out with guns and horses, searching the area for miles around. There was no sign of them. They had disappeared."

"And you think the lights were the highwaymen, going to their den?"

He nodded.

"Did you tell anyone about seeing them?"

"I told Roderick the next morning."

"Oh? Then he came back from his business trip."

"Sometime during the night. I don't know when. One of the servants came to find me. Laurel had awakened and missed me. The man wheeled me back and put me to bed. I had a chill and drank some brandy. It was after ten when I got up the next morning. Roderick was in his study."

"What did he say when you told him about the lights?"

"Nothing much. We didn't know about the attack until later."

"I see."

"And do you see why I would like you to leave Dower House?"

I forced myself to smile. "Your concern is sweet, Paul, but I am not frightened by highwaymen, or rumors of highwaymen. Even if it were true, if they were in the quarries, I fail to see how that could harm me. Dower House is mine, and nothing shall drive me away."

Paul Mellory did not say anything. He fumbled with the blanket, pulling it tighter about his knees. Paul was a fine boy, and I felt sure that he was sincere, but I knew that he admired his brother and that he was loyal. For a moment I wondered if Roderick Mellory had put him up to this, had told him to tell me about the lights and highwaymen, hoping that I would be frightened enough to agree to sell Dower House. Roderick knew that nothing he himself could say would influence me, but he also knew that I liked Paul and respected him. Perhaps he had hoped that his gentle brother would prove successful where he himself had failed.

"If the highwaymen are there," I said, "I am sure they will be found. They can't go on like this, striking and eluding the law. They'll be captured before long, and in the meantime I have my dog, Peter, and I have a revolver. Don't worry about me, Paul."

He looked up. There was an expression of deep concern in his eyes, and his brows were pressed into a tight frown. His cheeks were pale, and his thin lips were turned down at one corner. He stared at me for a moment, and then he smiled, slowly, the smile a mere flicker on his lips.

"You're indomitable," he said then. "I should have known you couldn't be frightened."

I had no time to think about these words, for Laurel Mellory came hurrying into the room. Her eyes were wide and her cheeks were tinged with the hot flush of excitement. She saw us and caught herself on her way through the room, breathing heavily.

"Oh! There you are, Angela. I've been looking everywhere. You've been gone so long, I thought you'd changed your mind and left with Greg. They're serving now—pheasant and glazed hams and juicy brown roasts and cakes—I have never seen so much food. Let's get our plates and eat, and then there are ever so many men who want to dance—Paul, are you coming?"

He looked at his sister and smiled. "No, I think I'll stay here for a while. You two go on."

"Can I bring you anything?" Laurel asked, disappointed.

"No, I'll get a plate later on."

"Very well. Come, Angela—"

The tables were spread with snowy white linen cloths, and there were gorgeous arrangements of bronze and gold flowers, but the real spectacle was the food itself. There were huge gold-rimmed platters heaped with every kind of food imaginable. There was a crisp suckling pig with an apple in its mouth, golden pheasant under glass, platters of oysters. Plates of exquisite china held stacks of beautiful pink and chocolate cakes, and a servant in rust-colored uniform was dishing out ice cream from a deep, silver-plated dish. Other servants, all in the rust uniforms, worked in a rush to slice the meats and fill the plates held out to them by the loud impatient crowd.

"Isn't it exciting!" Laurel exclaimed as we moved away with our heaping plates. "Oh, look, there's the mayor and his wife; she's the one in purple velvet with those white flowers. How greedy they are, using their elbows to get up to the table. And that's Albert Clinton, the little man in the shabby brown suit who is standing back with an empty plate. He owns Clinton Manor, a huge old estate in the next county. It's all run down, but he's too proud to do anything about it. It was cruel of Roderick, asking him here so that he could preen in front of the poor man. Oh, Angela, do you see that soldier with the short gold hair? He danced with me, and he said such nice things. I'm afraid he is already a little tipsy, but then the champagne is so heady, all those bubbles."

Laurel babbled on, thrilled and excited by everything around her. It was nice to see her so animated, but I thought how she would have to pay for this over-excitement later on with those severe headaches she suffered with. I had no doubt she would be in bed for days with a painful migraine, but I supposed these few hours of breathlessness were worth it for her. I was glad someone was enjoying the ball. Paul wasn't, and I doubted if Roderick Mellory really was, excepting his self-satisfaction. I certainly was not enjoying myself. My nostrils quivered with disapproval of all the waste and frivolity, but I tried not to let Laurel notice this.

After we had eaten, a young man came over and swept Laurel away to the strains of the music. In a moment the young soldier with golden hair asked me to dance. He was indeed tipsy, but he danced marvelously, his arm tight about my waist, his body moving with supple grace. He talked amusingly and whispered an indiscreet question in my ear. I merely laughed at him, smiling at his youthful enthusiasm. Everyone seemed to be dancing now. Couples crowded the floor, and I had lost sight of Laurel. A man with silver hair asked me to dance after the young soldier had left, and then another. I had no idea how long I danced, in the arms of one man after the other. It felt exhilarating to hold my head back, my eyes half closed, spinning around. My feet seemed winged, my body seemed without will, to be turned and whirled by the man who was leading me. For a while I thought about nothing but the music and the man who happened to be guiding me at the moment.

After what seemed like hours I began to tire, and I asked my partner to lead me over to one side of the room where people were standing, watching. A servant brought me a glass of champagne, and I did not have the will to refuse, although I was already giddy. I drank it too quickly and my head began to swim. I felt as if I were floating, suspended over the ballroom, seeing everything from a height. I knew that I needed fresh air. I made my way blindly to the French doors that opened onto the terrace and gardens, walking very carefully and in fear that I would stumble and fall.

It was very cool outside, but the fresh air felt wonderful. Moonlight poured over the tiled terrace, and everything seemed to be dark blue shadow and wavering silver. I took several deep breaths. My head stopped spinning around, and I could feel my equilibrium returning. A path led down to the formal gardens. There were tall box shrubs and carefully trimmed rose bushes. A white marble fountain stood in the center of a clearing, sprays of misty water billowing like plumes, and I moved toward it slowly. All this was washed in moonlight. It was calm and serenely beautiful after the bright flamboyance of the ballroom. A bird sang prettily from the bough of a tree and I stood lost in thought, listening to the warbling of the bird and wondering what Nan would say when I told her about this evening.

I did not hear footsteps. He must have come very quietly, deliberately making no noise. He might have been standing there for a long time, observing me, for when he spoke he was standing beside a trellis, one hand on the wisteria vine, the other jammed in his pocket. It was a casual pose. Perhaps he had been there all the time, even before I came.

"A perfect picture of maiden in moonlight," he said.

I whirled around, startled.

"No, no, don't move. You spoil the picture. You

look perfect just as you are, silhouetted against the fountain."

"How dare you frighten me like that," I snapped.

"I thought you were the woman who didn't frighten."

"Spare me your witticisms, Mr. Mellory."

"I see you are not wearing the dress I sent," he remarked, coming toward me in a lazy stride. "Did it not fit?" He laughed softly. "I thought I was rather good at judging a woman's dress size."

"You judged this woman wrong," I retorted.

"Really? I must say the dress you are wearing is quite nice. The color is very becoming, even in moonlight. Tell me, are you enjoying the ball?"

"I—it's very lavish." I hoped my voice showed my disdain.

"Indeed it is. You don't like lavish things?"

"I'm afraid not."

"The simple life for you. A little home in the country and the sounds of cocks crowing in the morning. Is that really your kind of thing, Miss Todd? I can imagine you in far more elegant surroundings."

"I see no point in discussing it with you."

"With what I would give you for Dower House you could have many elegant things. You could travel to Europe. You could wear fine gowns. You could become a young woman of fashion."

"I'm sure your offer is very generous, Mr. Mellory, but I've told you before that I have no intentions of selling Dower House."

"You and I are going to fight, you know," he said in a low voice.

"I'm prepared for that."

"I fight dirty."

"I'm prepared for that, too."

"You think you can win against me?"

"I shall try."

He was standing directly in front of me, his hands resting on his hips and his legs spread far apart. The jacket of his suit fell open, exposing the silver-stitched blue vest that fit tightly across his wide chest. He was staring into my eyes, his own filled with something dark that I could not read. I could not look away. I could not give him that satisfaction. For a long time we stood like that, then Roderick Mellory began to smile. I could hear the music from the distance, a soft, muted sound that was not as loud as the bird's song.

"I do admire your will," he said. "It's rare."

"Will you step aside, Mr. Mellory? I think I shall leave."

"Where is your escort—the gallant Mr. Ingram?"

"He had to leave. A child became ill at the school."

"I see. It seems I am always finding you without escorts," he said, referring to that day at the May Fete. "It seems a shame, an attractive and personable lady like you." He was working slowly now, trying to irritate me further. His voice was gentle, sincere, but the smile on his lips was cynical.

"Your sister said one of your carriages would take me home," I said.

"I will see to that—later."

"I would like to leave now," I replied, stressing the last word.

"But you are my guest," he said, his voice mocking, "and I must be a good host. You've seen the ballroom, you've tasted the food, and you've drunk the champagne, but you haven't danced with me yet."

"I'll gladly forgo that pleasure."

"But I won't," Roderick Mellory said, pulling me into his arms. With a quick series of motions he had propelled me into a dance, and I could not do anything but follow his lead. His arm was like a tight vise around my waist, and his free hand gripped my wrist. I struggled for a moment, helplessly, then, realizing the futility of my efforts, I let him do as he desired, whirling me around over the smooth surface of the ground. The music was far away, soft, but he moved in perfect time. Moonlight poured over us as we circled the fountain.

I closed my eyes, trying to resist the power of the man as best I was able. I moved rigidly, refusing to relax, and his arm tightened about my waist. "Relax," he whispered in my ear, "just relax," and in a moment I was relaxing, against my will, moving as he moved, swept away as in a trance. He was a wonderful dancer, masterful yet fluid in his movements. I felt his body against mine, and I felt his strength, and it seemed that I had no will, no being, no power to do anything but melt against him and be what he wanted me to be.

My head felt dizzy, and my wrists felt weak, and I tried to fight the sheer pleasure of the moment. I hate him, I hate him, I told myself, over and over, but another me, momentarily stronger, came alive, causing each nerve to tingle. I could not open my eyes. I could not catch my breath. I could only yield to the moment and savor it with all my body.

He stopped. I was too weak to move. I rested

against his chest for a moment, trying to pull myself together. Roderick Mellory put his hands on
my shoulders and pushed me away, gently.

"There," he said. "I've done my duty."

I could not speak, nor could I look up at him.

"You are an excellent partner," Roderick Mellory said. "A little like a Thoroughbred filly,
though. A Thoroughbred has too much spirit, and
the spirit must be broken before the true grace
will show."

"You haven't broken my spirit."

"Not entirely. Not yet."

"You are insufferably rude."

My voice trembled slightly. He had won. I had
given in when we were dancing, reluctantly allowing him his little victory. Reluctantly? I wondered. At first, yes, I had fought him, but later—I
refused to examine that too closely. I closed my
mind to it.

"You are trembling," he said.

I tried to still myself.

"Look up at me." It was an order.

I kept my eyes closed tightly, refusing to obey.
Roderick Mellory wrapped his fingers around
my chin and tilted my head up. I looked up at his
face through fluttering lashes. Every feature was
distinct in the moonlight. I saw the strangely attractive hump on his nose and the eyebrows, de-
monically arched over his eyes like dark wings. I
saw his smile, and my cheeks flushed hot with
shame. His smile was one of pure self-satisfaction. It was like a leer.

I drew away from him, anger replacing any
other emotions I might have felt.

"You are loathsome," I said. "Loathsome."

"And you are very young, very unwise."

"What they say about you is true. You are a devil."

"Don't make me fight you. Don't do that."

"A devil—" I repeated.

"I will hurt you. You won't like that."

"I don't believe you have the power to hurt me," I replied, as firmly as I could.

"No?" he asked, his voice gently mocking.

"No!" I retorted.

He pulled me into his arms, very casually, almost without interest in what he was doing, it seemed. He swung me around, fitting my body against his, one arm wrapped loosely about my waist, the other enfolding my shoulders. He held his face over mine, looking into my eyes. His own were dark and glittering with amusement. His lips curled into that ironic smile, and then they covered my mouth. It had all happened too quickly for me to struggle. After his lips began to move firmly over mine I lost any will to even try to resist him. I would have fallen but for his arms holding me against his body.

He released me abruptly. I staggered for a moment but managed to stand. He laughed quietly. I dared not look at his face again.

"I will send for a carriage, Miss Todd," he said. "It will be waiting for you in front in a few minutes. You can go home now."

Roderick Mellory left, sauntering away with his hands in his pockets. He continued to laugh quietly, and the sound rang in the quietness of the garden. I heard his footsteps pass across the tiled terrace, and there was a loud burst of music as he opened the French doors. I stood alone in the garden, surrounded by wavering moonlight and heavy blue shadows. The bird had stopped singing, and it was very still. There was only the sound of my own rapid, uneven breathing.

11

*T*he sky was the color of ashes. A stain of color began to spread on the horizon. I watched the faint orange penetrate the veils of gray. I had been sitting here at the window for hours, still in my ball gown, looking out at the night. A cock crowed in the distance, far away, a mournful sound, I thought. Peter lay curled at my feet, sleeping soundly, his silver coat all sleek and glossy from the bath Nan had given him last night. She was asleep when I came in, and I had not awakened her. I had not felt like talking. I had not felt like sleeping. I had sunk into the chair by the window, glad of the darkness and silence.

The darkness was going now. It had rained during the night and now fine veils of mist hung over the ground, like shrouds, I thought. The trees were tall, skeletal figures, half hidden by the mist. The cock crowed again and the light changed from orange to gold, penetrating the mist. I saw a farmer going slowly down the road, leading his cow, and three men with hoes walked across a field, moving slowly and lethargically at this early hour. I heard a banging noise in the kitchen and knew that Nan must be up. My solitude had ended, and I was sorry for that.

Peter stirred uncomfortably in his sleep and then raised his head, looking up at me with large, thoughtful eyes. I stroked his head. I knew without consulting a mirror that my cheeks were wan, my face colorless. My gown was crushed and rumpled from my night vigil, but I did not care. I would not ever wear it again. I stood up, bracing myself on the chair, surprised that I had the energy to move. I felt depleted. Even the slight task of getting out of the chair seemed to take more energy than I possessed. I stood for a moment, swaying a little as I felt the blood rushing through my numb body.

Nan came into the room, rubbing her eyes sleepily. A white lace cap was perched precariously over her tousled gold curls. When she saw me, a little cry escaped her lips, and she hurried to my side. She started to ask a dozen questions, but I raised my hand up in protest. She knew that questions would be futile, and she grew very calm, even dictatorial in an effort to take the situation in hand.

"You must get in bed—that lovely dress, all rumpled like that! How could you—and rest up. Your face is as white as, I don't know what. I am going to make a pot of coffee and some breakfast; we have ham, and I'll scramble some eggs. Now you go on up and change."

"I'm all right, Nan. Don't be so bossy. Breakfast

sounds lovely. I will be all right after I have some food."

"Whatever happened?"

"I came home. I didn't feel like sleeping. I sat up, watched the sun come up."

"Well, I must say . . ."

"Don't say anything. Just hurry with that coffee."

Nan's boisterous attitude and her lively comments helped me to brace up. After all, I told myself, life would go on. I had had an argument with Greg, and I had made a fool of myself before Roderick Mellory. I had spent half the night thinking about it, feeling humiliated, then angrily upbraiding myself, then feeling hurt, then puzzled. Continuing to brood about it could do me no good. I could not forget what had happened, but I certainly had better sense than to let it throw me into a fit of dejection. I would solve the problem of Greg somehow, and there would be another encounter with Roderick Mellory. The next time I would show him.

I brushed my hair angrily, thinking of the Master of Phoenix Hall. Spots of color came into my cheeks, and good, healthy anger made even the lack of sleep unimportant. As I walked down the stairs the tangy smells of coffee and ham made me feel even better. I felt full of life and energy, thoroughly revived. Activity, much activity, would be the best thing for me today. I quickened my step, full of good intentions. I would clean out the cupboards, wax and polish the floor, and perhaps, if there was time, I could do some weeding in the garden. If I kept busy enough, there would be no time to think.

Nan was bursting with all the questions I had

not allowed her to ask earlier. We sat at the table, eating the slices of thick, juicy ham and the fluffy yellow eggs she had cooked. After a cup of the steaming coffee I felt more like satisfying some of Nan's curiosity, but only some. She was primarily interested in the people and the dancing, and I gave her a much abridged account of the evening, merely by saying that Greg had been called away and that Laurel Mellory had furnished a carriage for the ride home. I told her about Lady Miriam Alton, and her eyes grew wide with amazement when I described Lady Miriam's gown and her jewels.

"She's a notorious hussy," Nan commented. "It would serve Mellory right if she bagged him. What a scandal, her married and all! Wouldn't it be glorious if they ran away together?"

"And what did you do last night?" I asked a little later.

"I bathed Peter. He gave such howls, but isn't his coat shiny? And, oh yes, Billy Johnson came to call. We—uh—took a walk." This last was said rather evasively. "That Billy Johnson! He gets fresher every time I see him!"

She spread strawberry jam on a biscuit, preferring to dismiss Billy Johnson from the conversation, but I noticed the twinkle in her eyes and the sly little smile on her lips. I wondered just what had happened during that walk.

I took a sip of my coffee. Ironically, it seemed I had never felt better in my life. From where I sat I could look through the window and see part of the granite quarry behind the house. The sun had completely evaporated the mists now and it sparkled and glittered on the sharp gray stones. There was certainly nothing forbidding about the

quarry this morning. I thought about what Paul
Mellory had said, and I was suddenly filled with
an irresistible urge to explore all those quarries
he had spoken of. It was a dazzling beautiful day,
and the sunshine and exercise would do me good,
I reasoned.

"Nan," I said, "we've never explored the quarries."

"Who'd want to?" she said without enthusiasm.
"I see enough of it every day—ugly pit of a thing
with all those rocks."

"But there are others," I said.

"Of course. More of the same thing. Spoiling
the countryside."

"Wouldn't it be nice to get out of the house for a
while? We could take Peter with us. It's such a
lovely day."

"I thought we were going to polish the floors
and straighten up the cupboards?"

"We can do that anytime. Where's your spirit of
adventure?"

Nan looked up at me sharply. She must know
that this sudden desire of mine to explore the
quarries was not usual. She probably suspected
an ulterior motive, but she decided to indulge me.
I did not want to go tracking off alone, and her
lively company would make the jaunt pleasant instead of arduous.

The sky was a luminous white, only slightly
washed with blue, as we skirted the quarry behind Dower House. Peter ran on ahead, barking
lustily as he scampered over the vivid green grass
that grew down to the edge of the pit. I had really
had no idea how large the quarry was before. It
loomed below us, a great vast pit like a wound in
the earth. Some of the gray rocks were tinted with

violet and blue, crusted with radiant chunks of mica. We were on the far side now. Across the yawning chasm Dower House looked very small, like some child's toy perched there, surrounded by tiny trees and small patches of garden.

"It looks so snug," I said. "So peaceful."

Nan nodded in reply, standing beside me. The wind whipped about us and caused our skirts to flutter about our legs. I looked at Dower House for a long time, my heart filled with the joy and pride of ownership. It was all mine, the only thing in the world I had, and no one would ever be able to take it away from me. Nan shared my emotions. The place meant almost as much to her as it did to me.

"Do you ever think about London?" I asked quietly.

"Not if I can help it," Nan retorted.

"Do you remember that day Mr. Patterson came into the shop? That day changed everything."

"I remember it well."

"It seems so long ago, doesn't it? So much has happened since then and our lives have changed so much."

"Well," she said, not caring for this sentimental reverie, "we're a lot busier now, and you, Miss Angel, are a lot flightier, sitting up all night and then wantin' to run all over the countryside like a colt! I swear, it perplexes me!"

"It's perfectly—"

"One would almost think," she snapped, interrupting me, "that you were in love."

"Nan! That's absurd."

"Is it?"

"Come along now. We have a lot more to see."

We walked on for almost half a mile. The quarry behind Dower House diminshed in size, grew narrow. We lost it completely for a while as we passed through a small wooded area. It was dark and shadowy, only a few wavering bars of sunlight falling through the roof of green and brown foliage above. We had to cross a small stream, and we stepped carefully over the flat rocks. The water gurgled pleasantly and there was the smell of moss and thick mud. Peter leaped over a rotten log, slimy with moss, and lunged at a squirrel on the other side, barking furiously as the tiny animal scurried up a tree and scolded him from a limb high above.

"He's certainly enjoying this," I remarked.

"I'm glad someone is," Nan snapped.

"Don't be so grumpy. The exercise is good for all of us."

"I've scratched my arm," she said, "and look at this." She held up her yellow skirt, examining a large tear in the material where she had caught it on a thorn.

"Perhaps it's the company that displeases you," I said, teasingly. "I'm sure you'd find it more enjoyable if Billy Johnson were with you."

"Miss Angel!" she said, shocked. But she didn't complain anymore.

On the other side of the woods there was a hill sloping down gently to the edge of another quarry. The grass was thick and luxuriantly green and thousands of buttercups were scattered in bright spots of yellow over the hill. The quarry was narrow here, gradually widening and becoming deeper as we moved along. Far off, across the quarry, there was another wooded area, and beyond I could see the roof of Phoenix Hall spreading majestically over the tops of the trees.

"This quarry connects with the one behind Dower House," I said, "although you can't tell it. Look, see how this rock has a pinkish shade? It's slightly different from the other. If you look carefully, you can see the caves and tunnels down there. See where the shadows are? Some of the caves were made by the men who worked in the quarries, some of them are natural, washed away by the sea centuries ago."

"I don't care to stand that close to the edge," Nan said. "You be careful, Miss Angel. Those rocks are slippery. If you fell—"

"Nonsense. I'm not going to fall."

We walked on for a long time. I peered down at the quarries. I could see now why they would furnish such a good hiding place: vast, rugged, rock filled, affording any number of places for concealment, and there were also great yawning holes in the side of the earth that opened like dark mouths, tunnels leading into labyrinths of connecting caves. Someone had said that some of the caves went down half a mile into the earth.

"It does look dangerous, doesn't it?" I said, standing at the edge of the quarry.

"It looks downright spooky. A person could get lost and never be found down there."

I agreed, nodding my head.

"Do you know about the highwaymen's attack the other night?" she said in a quiet voice.

"Paul Mellory told me," I replied. "How did you find out about it?"

"Billy was part of the search party. He rode around half the night, swinging his lantern and shouting at shadows. He said they're sure about the highwaymen having a den somewhere in the quarries. You knew that?"

"Yes."

"So that's why you wanted to come?"

"Not really," I replied evasively.

"Miss Angel, do you remember those lights we saw?"

"Of course."

"It gives me the creeps," she said, folding her arms about her.

"Don't be silly, Nan. If they do have a hideout somewhere in these quarries you can be sure it's not near Dower House or anyplace where there are people living. They'd be foolish to run the risk of being seen."

"But those lights—"

"Probably a farmer looking for a stray calf."

The explanation sounded weak even to me, but I did not want to alarm Nan, and I spoke the words for my own benefit as well. I did not like all the things that had been happening, and I was glad we had Peter to keep us company at the house. As I stood looking down at the quarries I resolved to examine the little gun I had found in Aunt Lucille's drawer more closely and also to learn how to shoot it.

We might have been gone for two or three hours when the weather went into one of those abrupt changes so typical of Cornwall in late spring and early summer. Clouds had begun to skim across the surface of the white sky and a suddenly brisk breeze caused the grass at our feet to undulate like miniature waves. The clouds banked up, changing from white to gray and gradually to black. Soon the whole sky was crowded with great lumbering black clouds that rolled like whales on a stormy sea. The wind turned fierce, whipping at us with stinging force. I could smell the tangy smell of the salty air blowing from a nearby channel that came in from the coast, and a solitary sea gull went soaring overhead, screaming in anguish as he fought the wind.

We could not possibly get back to Dower House before it rained. There was a large wooded area beyond the next clearing and we hurried towards it with Peter leading the way. The countryside, so lovely a short time ago, seemed to have been drained of color. Everything was tinged with gray and the woods ahead looked dark, the trees black outlines. They would give us some shelter from the wind and rain. We ran quickly. I stumbled once and would have fallen if Nan hadn't caught my arm. We reached the woods, out of breath and panting, huddling under the thick arms of a great oak which stood on the edge of the clearing.

The rain fell heavily for a while, blinding sheets of rain that blotted out everything. Nan and I leaned against the trunk of the trees, relatively dry, although rain dripped down from the boughs overhead. Peter shivered at my feet, whimpering as thunder drummed loudly. Flashes of lightning illuminated the clearing in front of us and I could see puddles of mud. I did not mind the rain. Safely under the tree, I felt rather awed by this exhibition of nature's fury. It was but another part of the country that I had grown to love since I had come to Cornwall.

After a while the rain diminished into a fine, light mist and the clouds rolled away, leaving a wet gray sky that glowed with a curious greenish tint. The field in front of us was a sodden mass and the quarries beyond were ugly, all dark gray and black in the light. The air itself seemed to borrow a cast of faint green from the sky. It was a world completely changed, almost eerie now with the unrelieved gray and green and black.

Nan wiped away a damp tendril of hair that had plastered itself against her temple. We were both a little damp, with dark splotches on our clothes where rain had stained them. Peter stood shaking drops of water from his silver coat. His paws were muddy and he looked up at me with reproachful eyes. I pulled a piece of bark from the tree, hesitant to start back in all that mud, and it was then that we heard the shouting.

It came from the other side of the woods. The voices were distinct, although we could not make out any of the words. Then a man rode across the field, his horse kicking up splurts of muddy water. He was but a silhouette in the light, but Nan grabbed my hand, squeezing it tightly. I thought at first that the gesture had been one of terror, but her face showed not a bit of alarm, merely intense excitement.

"That was Billy!" she cried. "Whatever is he doing? What is all that shouting? Oh, Miss Angel, let's go see."

"Are you sure it was Billy?"

"Of course. Don't you think I know Billy Johnson when I see him? Something dreadful has happened, Miss Angel, I just know it!"

The woods spread out for several hundred yards and then ended abruptly. The quarry that had been in front of us when we were under the oak tree made a gradual curve, spreading out to form a natural ravine at the side of the woods. Nan and I hurried around the trees, ignoring the mud that splattered the hems of our dresses. When we cleared the woods we could see a knot of men on a hill some distance away. There were several horses and a carriage. Billy was just dismounting, leaping off his horse to say something to one of the men. The men were making excited gestures and pointing down into the ravine. As we neared the gathering, Peter barked loudly, and the men looked up, no doubt astounded to see two women out in the countryside so soon after a storm.

They all fell silent, looking grim and secretive, moving closer about the carriage and watching us with worried eyes. I recognized the local constable and two of the men who were his assistants. There was a farmer in a battered hat, a mournful expression on his face. He stood with his hoe in hand, apparently bewildered. His young son stood cowering behind his father's legs, his eyes wide with fright. Billy Johnson stood beside the constable, and another man stood a little apart, looking down at the ravine.

He turned around, and I saw that it was Roderick Mellory. He wore tall black boots and a black cape that whipped about his shoulders. He looked at me with dark eyes, his face like a mask.

"What has happened?" Nan cried, hurrying to Billy.

"You all shouldn't be here," Billy said, his voice solemn. "What are you doing out here?"

"We went for a walk and got caught in the rain. We heard the shouting. What's happened, Billy?"

Billy was uncommunicative, standing with his arms folded and looking very sober and masculine. Nan was infuriated, but she knew that she could not handle him when he was in such a mood and she fell silent. Whatever had happened was something they wished to keep from us. There was an atmosphere of male conspiracy and they all treated us like unwelcome intruders. Tension hung in the air, heavy like something tangible over our heads, ready to explode at any moment.

Roderick Mellory continued to stare at me. I was very conscious of my mud-splattered blue dress and my damp hair. I stood with my hand resting on Peter's head, trying to still him. The Master of Phoenix Hall was not really a part of this group. He stood apart, his cloak whipping about his shoulders like furious black wings. Alone, standing on the edge of the ravine, he still dominated. The men glanced at him uneasily, not wanting to say or do anything that would not meet with his approval.

"I suppose we'll have to tell them?" the constable said, and Roderick Mellory nodded solemnly, still staring at me.

"Is something wrong?" I asked, the words sounding foolish even to me. I knew something was wrong. I could feel it all around me, and I felt suddenly very cold, afraid of what the constable would tell me.

"There's been a—an accident," he said. "Young Kip was out looking for a ewe that had strayed. He was hunting in the ravine and almost stumbled over the man—the body."

"Someone is dead?" I said, looking at the frightened child.

"Kip rushed back to the farm and told his father, and his father drove into town to get us. Mr. Mellory and Johnson here came along to help identify the body. We believe we know who he is.

He isn't one of the Lockwood lads, that's for sure. Johnson has just returned from summoning the doctor. We don't want to do anything until he arrives and has a look."

"He's—down there?" Nan asked, her eyes wide.

Billy nodded in reply. Nan stepped to the edge of the ravine. I saw her shoulders grow rigid, and when she turned around her face was very pale. She rushed straight to Billy, and he put his arms around her protectively. I could not help myself. I had to look. The constable put his hand on my arm, trying to restrain me, but I shook it off, determined to see for myself.

The man was sprawled out only a few yards below. His arms and legs were flung out over the rocks. His eyes were wide open, staring sightlessly up at me, and his face had frozen into a shape of pure terror, the mouth wide and the lips pulled back over the teeth as though he had died with a scream tearing from his throat. One hand still grasped a black mask and the other held a few gold sovereigns. There were several gold pieces scattered around over the rocks near him, glittering brightly in the dim gray-green light. A knife protruded from the man's chest.

I don't know how long I looked. I felt a dizzy sensation, as though I were about to fall, and I closed my eyes, feeling my body grow weak. Strong hands clasped my shoulders, pulling me back. I rested against a firm body, trying to overcome the whirling black wings that threatened to close over my brain, and in a moment I was able to stand without support.

"That was a foolish thing to do," Roderick Mellory said, releasing me. He looked into my eyes. I thought I read concern in his expression, and his voice had certainly been gentle.

"It's one of them, all right," the constable said. "They've had a falling out. This one probably tried to take more than his share. There is no honor among thieves, despite what people might think. They've been strong up till now, sly and wary, but they're beginning to split. That's a good sign. We'll catch them now, for sure, and soon."

I hardly heard his words. None of this was real. It was a nightmare. I would wake to find that none of it had happened. The mist still fell, fine, sharp needles burning our cheeks, and the faint green light glowed over the grim faces of the men, and over what was below. There was no sun. There was no beauty. There was only this ugly thing that had happened, and it was real. I knew that. I knew it would be impossible for me ever to forget what I had seen, no matter how often I awoke.

Roderick Mellory stepped over to the carriage. When he returned he had a small flask of brandy. He unscrewed the silver top and forced me to drink some of the burning liquid. I shook my head in protest, but he insisted and I saw that it would be futile to resist. I could feel the liquor burning inside me, and as the warmth spread some of the dizziness left. He took the flask and put its top back on, never saying a word.

"Then they're definitely holed up in the quarry?" one of the men asked.

The constable nodded. "This makes it a dead certainty. They're in here somewhere, and we'll find them. It's only a matter of time. We've searched before, but they were too clever for us.

Things have changed now. They are getting careless. We'll get them," he said with finality.

Roderick Mellory took my elbow and led me to the carriage. He motioned to Nan and she came and opened the door, helping me in. There was a road just ahead. It wound around the outskirts of the village and back to Phoenix Hall. Nan held my hand tightly as we rode, and I was aware of nothing but the joggling motion of the vehicle and the feeling of extreme exhaustion. The carriage stopped in front of Dower House and we got out, Roderick Mellory not speaking as he held the door open for us. He climbed back up on his seat and drove away and I watched the carriage disappear with feelings even more mixed and confusing than those I had felt in the garden the night before.

12

*T*he next day was bright and busy. Nan and I did all the things I had postponed the day before. We waxed the kitchen floor until it gleamed with a golden sheen. Nan polished all the copper pots, humming to herself, while I cleaned out the cupboards. There was a bustle in the house as we moved from one part to another with energetic activity. I re-tacked the carpet on the stairs, driving the tacks in with a tiny hammer, and Nan starched and ironed all the curtains. The canary chirped contentedly in the parlor and Peter rested in front of the hearth, a little nervous at all this noise and activity.

It was after noon when Billy arrived in his wagon. I was standing on a small ladder, hanging the freshly ironed curtains. Nan was putting the finishing touches on the furniture, whisking about with a feather duster. We were both tired, but it was a contented tiredness, comfortable. Billy brought some fertilizer for the garden and he spread it out with a rake while Nan and I finished the last chores. When we had finished we stepped outside to watch while Billy spread the last shovelful.

"There," he said, leaning against the handle of the rake. "That'll do it." He looked up at us with a broad smile, contented with a job well done. Nan studied him with admiration, her hands on her hips. Billy wore a sleeveless leather jerkin and tight pants faded of any color. His light brown hair, damp now with perspiration, was already a little bleached from the sun, and his arms were bronzed. He had the look of a healthy animal, magnificent in strength. Only his penny-colored eyes were gentle as they looked at Nan.

"All finished with your work?" he asked her.

"Just about," she replied, studiedly indifferent.

"Got any plans for the rest of the afternoon?"

"Not unless Miss Angel has something else she wants done."

I shook my head. Nan's face had that look of pleased anticipation. She and Billy would spend the rest of the afternoon together, flirting, quarreling, being carefree. How easy it is for them to forget all else when they are with each other, I thought.

"You smell of manure," Nan said as Billy put up the rake.

"You smell of beeswax and lemon," he replied, "and you've got a bit of dirt on the tip of your nose."

"Why don't you go off," she said. "You're no prize, you know. I have other things to do this afternoon. I may not want you lugging about the place, getting in the way."

"If you don't want me I can go find Mary Anne

Munsey. She'll not be so impudent, you can bet on that."

They argued playfully for a few minutes, both enjoying it immensely as they exchanged little insults and poked one another. They were like two children just turned out of school, and I felt suddenly very lonely as I stood there in the garden. I looked at the bright nasturtiums, red and yellow in their neat beds. The manure that Billy had spread steamed a little, filling the garden with a pungent odor.

"I think I'll bake some bread," Nan said. "You might keep me company in the kitchen, Billy Johnson. There are some knives that need to be sharpened, and you could make yourself useful while you're lounging. Later on we might go for a stroll, but only if you behave yourself."

The afternoon stretched ahead of me. It must be filled somehow. I did not want to rest. I did not want to stop and give myself any time to think and brood. Billy's wagon was standing in front of the house. I decided to borrow it and drive in to Lockwood. It had been a long time since I had been to the village and a long, leisurely drive would be good for me. There was really nothing I needed in the way of provisions, but I could look at material in the dry goods store and later stop by and see Greg at the school. I had not seen him since the night of the ball, and I wanted very much to talk to him.

Nan and Billy were laughing merrily in the kitchen when I left. They would not even notice my absence, I thought. I had changed into a dress of white cotton, printed with tiny pink and green flowers, and I wore a broadbrimmed white straw sun bonnet with dangling green ribbons, feeling rather festive in my fresh attire. Billy's old dappled-gray horse moved slowly down the road. I held the reins loosely in my hand, letting the animal take his time. The limbs of the trees stretched overhead, and sunlight sifted through the rich green canopy to dapple the road with spots of yellow.

It was peaceful and lovely today, making yesterday's nightmare seem all the more improbable. I had put it out of my mind as best I could. It would be foolish to dwell on the event, far better to forget it as soon as I could. It did not concern me. They would catch the highwaymen, and I would go on living in my house, tending my garden, enjoying the serenity and solitude of the place.

I averted my eyes as I passed Phoenix Hall. I did not want to look at it and be reminded. I wanted to forget. It seemed so unfair that my life here in Cornwall must be spoiled by the man who lived in that house. I thought of all the things he had done to plague me and it seemed almost too much to bear. He had tried to buy Dower House and then he had tried to frighten me away, and that had not worked either. I wondered what he would try next. Once the prospect of a good fight with him caused me to quicken with excitement. I had been ready to exchange sharp remarks, to match my wits against his, but I no longer even felt up to that.

Driving on, I saw a field of wild poppies on one side of the road. The flowers were tattered balls of golden orange, with deep red centers, and their odor was intoxicating, heady, making me almost drowsy. Above, the sky unfurled like a bolt of watered blue silk. The wagon jogged along the road, the gray's hooves stirring up little clouds of dust. The intense sun had already evaporated every sign of yesterday's rain.

I clicked the reins, a little anxious to get to the village. I wanted to talk to Greg. I wanted to tell him what had happened and hear his soothing voice tell me that it would all be all right. I wanted to see his gentle eyes and feel the protection of his presence. Our quarrel the night of the ball seemed utterly nonsensical now. It was hard to remember what it had all been about. Greg was wise. I needed his wisdom. He was confused. He needed my understanding. He had been very tired that night, and worried about his student. It was only natural that he be a little fretful. I wanted to see him and make amends.

The wagon rumbled over a small wooden bridge that spanned a stream. Two little boys sat on the bank below, under the shade of an oak tree, their bamboo poles dangling in the water. One of the poles jerked violently and the boy holding it pulled the line in, yelling with glee as a fat silver fish thrashed on the surface of the water. I smiled, happy. A world that held such innocence, such pure joy as that I had seen in the face of that child, could be no place for melancholy, and I drove on with lightened spirits.

Lockwood was brimming with activity as it usually was. Two donkeys were tethered in a vacant lot, braying loudly as a band of children ran about them. A group of men were holding an auction in the square, their weathered faces seamed with concentration as they listened to the bids and made their own. A husky lad in dusty clothes pushed a barrow heaped with cabbage and carrots towards the market, pursued by a furiously barking brown and white dog that snapped at his heels. I left Billy's wagon in front of the tiny post office and strolled towards the dry goods store, pausing to examine some exquisite handmade lace that a wrinkled old woman displayed at a battered wooden booth.

Two shabby children stood in front of the bakery and candy store, their dirty faces pressed against the glass. They peered in at the stacks of tiny frosted cakes and the jars of colored rock candy, longing for the impossible. I impulsively took out some coins and placed them in the grubby little hands. Their eyes grew wide with incredulity at this sudden windfall, and they hesitated only a moment before racing inside.

The dry goods store was busy, but I was in no hurry. Farm women handled the coarse, sturdy materials that would suffice for their family's clothes. A young girl stood dreamily examining strands of brightly colored ribbons. Village women looked at buttons and laces and bonnets, and all those who had no intentions of buying lingered to exchange gossip. This was the one place in Lockwood where the women would talk unabashedly about things their husbands might disapprove of their discussing. All the talk today was about the highwaymen and the body that had been found in the ravine, and I heard rather startling theories.

I spoke to no one. I was still an outsider. I examined bolts of bright printed cloth, paying more heed to what was being said than to the yards of cotton and linen I was handling. I learned that the dead man had lived near Devon and had been rarely seen in Lockwood. I heard that a group of officers from Scotland Yard was expected to ar-

rive soon and that surveillance of the area had
increased three times in strength. It was generally
agreed that the bandits would be caught soon, if
they had not already left the county. There was
much speculation about who the "connection" in
Lockwood could be. He had to be someone who
had access to private information about finances
and transport.

I head Roderick Mellory's name mentioned.

It would be so easy to believe, I thought. I
would have liked to believe it. He was an unscrupulous man. In his position he undoubtedly had
access to all the information the highwaymen
would need to know when and where to strike.
He had certainly obtained a great deal of money
just recently, or else he would not have been able
to finance the repairs and embellishments at
Phoenix Hall. He had certainly not been above
trying to frighten me away from Dower House.
Would a man who would not stop at terrorizing a
defenseless woman stop at robbery—and murder?

It was foolish speculation on my part. I did not
like the man, but I could not afford to let my personal feelings color my reasoning. The men and
women of Lockwood had many reasons for de-
testing Roderick Mellory, but he *was* Roderick
Mellory, one of Cornwall's genuine aristocrats,
and as such he was surely above suspicion.

As I left the store I heard another woman building a case against the local Catholic Abbot, listing
motives and means, and I realized then just how
foolish my thoughts were. When something like
this happened in a village the size of Lockwood, it
would be easy for hysteria to prevail, and no
doubt many personal grudges would be taken out

and aired. That was all the more reason to remain calm and objective.

It was just a short walk from the dry goods store to the school. The sun was beginning its gradual decline, gilding the roofs with white gold and reflecting dazzling sunbursts from the bronze steeple of the Protestant Church. I knew that the school would be closed for the weekend, but I hoped Greg would be in his office. He spent much of his spare time there working on assignments, studying, grading papers. The schoolhouse looked deserted when I reached it. It was a large redstone building with well worn white marble steps and a small, dingy portico. There was a shabby bed of delphiniums in front, their blue petals limp, and the grass was already brown and patchy, well trodden by careless young feet.

There was no answer when I knocked on the huge front door. I rapped the tarnished brass lion's head against the oak, standing there under the portico and listening to the pigeons cooing. Still there was no answer. Greg's office was in back of the building, in one of the wings, and if he was there he probably would not be able to hear my knocking. I tried the door handle. It was not locked and the door swung open heavily, groaning a little on its hinges. The main hall was a vast tunnel of shadows, the only light coming from a small window at the other end where another led to the wings on either side of the building.

I hesitated for a moment. I felt like an intruder. I could see an umbrella stand, a pair of discarded galoshes beside it, and an empty coat rack. The silence was heavy, so intense that I could hear myself breathing. I wanted to see Greg very badly. I felt I had to talk to him. If he was in his office he would not mind my coming in like this, and if he was not no one would know I had been here. I cleared my throat, looking down the long dark hall.

I knew that it was silly to just stand there. I had come in to Lockwood especially to see Greg, and it would be ridiculous to go away now because no one had answered my knock. I squared my shoulders and began to walk down the hall. The heels of my shoes tapped loudly on the tiles. The noise echoed all around me. I had the curious feeling that the very walls of the empty school were watching me and listening, just waiting for some kind of signal to spring to life. It was an eerie sensation. I supposed it was typical of all old buildings ordinarily filled with activity, but it was a bit unnerving just the same.

I hesitated at the end of the hall, trying to remember in which wing of the building Greg's office was located. Now that my footsteps were not ringing on the tiles, the silence seemed even more oppressive. Light leaked in faintly from the window, showing me rows of doors, all of them closed. A boy had left a satchel of books on the floor, a dark blue school cap resting on top of them. I could smell chalk dust and the smell of ink and leather and bodies, mixed with the sharp, acrid odor of an apple that some child had left in his desk and long since forgotten.

"Greg," I called. My voice sounded faint and timid.

There was no reply but an echo that rang for a moment and then died. I caught my breath. It was foolish to be frightened, yet I felt that something was waiting for me, something unpleasant. It was cool here inside, the air stale, untouched by the sun, and I felt a chill rise up my spine. I felt suddenly weak, unable to move. It was impossible to turn back and go down that hall towards the door where I had entered. It was equally impossible to go looking for Greg's office down these long corridors.

I was admonishing myself for this silly apprehension when I heard the door opening. It came from somewhere down the hall leading to the library. The door was creaking on its hinges as though it was being opened slowly, stealthily. Although there were windows down this intersecting hall, they were set high up and afforded very little light. The shadows were thick, and they seemed to move. The creaking stopped and I heard footsteps. Someone was coming down the hall towards me, moving slowly and cautiously and keeping close to the wall where the light would not reveal him.

I was frozen, too frightened to even cry out. I leaned against the wall, under the window, waiting. The footsteps came nearer, then they stopped. I could feel a pair of eyes studying me.

"Miss Todd?"

I looked up. The man had stopped a few yards away. The light showed his face, and it was as startled as my own must have been. I recognized the man as Mr. Stephenson, Greg's colleague. His eyebrows were lifted in surprise and his lips were parted. I noticed that he was clutching a small bronze figurine as though it were a bludgeon.

"Whatever are you doing here?" he asked. His voice was shaky. It was obvious that he was as unnerved as I had been.

"Mr. Stephenson—you gave me such a fright. I came to see Greg—Mr. Ingram. I thought he would be working in his office. No one answered my knock, but the door was open. I came on in."

"I see." He was plainly relieved. "I thought I heard someone knocking, but I couldn't imagine what anyone would want at this hour. I assumed it was my imagination."

"I'm sorry if I gave you a start."

"You gave me more than that, my dear young woman. I was ready to hit someone over the head with this Apollo." He looked down at the figurine in his hand. "Well, it seems we've both been shaken up. You are quite pale, Miss Todd. It couldn't have been very pleasant hearing someone stalk you down the hall." He smiled faintly.

"It wasn't," I assured him, returning the smile. "Is Mr. Ingram in his office?"

"Didn't you know? He had to return to Liverpool, or so he said. His brother seems to have undone all the good he accomplished on the first trip down."

"I didn't know," I said, feeling rather hurt that Greg had not told me. "When did he leave?"

"Yesterday morning. Quite early. Before dawn, in fact. His brother must be quite a case; surprising when Ingram himself is such a fine young person—high ideals. If he had any sense he would let the man stew in his own porridge, but I suppose family loyalty is admirable."

"Did he say when he would be returning to Lockwood?"

"In a day or so, he hoped."

"Well, I suppose it was urgent. That's why he didn't have time to inform me. I really came to inquire about the boy, Mr. Stephenson. How is he?"

"The boy? What are you talking about?"

"The lad who was taken ill night before last. Greg was very upset. He left Mr. Mellory's ball in order to come see about the child."

"There has been no illness in the school," Mr. Stephenson said. He looked at me curiously, as though I were making up the episode.

I did not wish to pursue the matter. If Greg had lied to me, there must have been a good reason for it. I doubted seriously if he had gone to Liverpool because of his brother. More than likely his sudden departure had something to do with the mysterious business transaction he had been so excited about the night of the ball.

"Perhaps I was mistaken," I said. "I must have misunderstood him. I hope you will forgive me my intrusion, Mr. Stephenson. I feel I owe you an apology."

"Please forget it, Miss Todd."

"I wonder if I could go to Mr. Ingram's office for a few minutes? There is a book he promised to lend me, and I would like to leave him a note. Would it be an inconvenience to you?"

"Of course not. I'll show you the way."

Mr. Stephenson led me down the hall and pointed out Greg's office. The door was locked, but he had a master key that opened it. I felt even more like an intruder as I watched the staid little man opening the door, but I felt I had to leave a note and I did want to borrow Greg's copy of *Jane Eyre*.

"I will be in the library if you need me," Mr. Stephenson said, holding the door open.

"I'll only be a few minutes. I'll find my way out. Please don't let me bother you anymore."

Mr. Stephenson nodded his head, looking at me again with that curious expression. He walked on down the hall, and I stood in the office, listening to his footsteps dying away. The shade was pulled up high, and the last rays of sunlight poured into the small room, revealing an oak bookcase crammed with books and pamphlets, a work table, a sturdy desk and a shabby easy chair upholstered in dark blue. There was a well worn magenta carpet on the floor and an assorted collection of framed engravings on the wall.

I felt uneasy. It was wrong to invade Greg's private domain like this while he was away, and I felt disonest, but now that I was here my curiosity would not let me leave. The room reflected the man, neat, orderly, dignified, a little worn but revealing cultured taste. I browsed over the book case and found a copy of the Brontë novel. I took it out and went over to the desk to write the note.

There was a green felt ink blotter on the desk, an onyx pen set, a chunk of quartz holding down a stack of student papers. I did not see a tablet or any writing paper, so I opened the top drawer, feeling just a tinge of guilt. There was no tablet. There were more student papers and a notebook filled with columns and columns of figures, with dates beside each entry. I supposed this was the book he kept to list student fees or something of the sort.

The second drawer held the tablet I was looking for, but I did not take it out. Instead, I took out Aunt Lucille's notebooks. There was a sheaf of papers on top, clipped together and covered with Greg's handwriting. I wondered if he had possibly broken the code. I spread the papers out over the desk and sat down, leaning my elbows on the desk and reading the closely written pages.

I do not know how long I may have read. The

sunlight that came through the windows took on a vivid orange glow and then began to fade, and outside the heavy veils of twilight began to fall, blurring everything together in a haze of blue. There was barely enough light left for me to see by. I sat there at the desk, trying to put my thoughts in order. A flood of hysteria threatened to overcome me. I knew I could not let that happen.

I turned through the pages of the notebooks, rereading various entries scrawled messily in black ink. At first I had not understood the references to money taken in, to time schedules, to various roads and villages. They had been interspersed with tedious essays about the properties of herbs and rather amusing anecdotes about the peculiarities of the people who came to see my aunt about potions and powders.

Later on, towards the last, it became all too evident what my aunt's real activies were.

January 21st.   He thinks he can cheat me. He should know better. He thinks I've done all this for a lark. He thinks I'm an eccentric old woman without moral standards who finds an outlet in all this. He really believes I am as dotty as they say I am. I'm a harmless old woman who fools around with herbs and crazy cures. That's what they all say, and that's his protection. They would never suspect I had anything to do with this business. Without me he hasn't a chance to pull it off. If I were to talk . . . but he won't dare cross me.

I wondered what "all this" was about. It became increasingly clear as I read on.

January 30th.   He says his position protects
him. They wouldn't dare connect him with the
robberies. If only they knew what a devil he
really is! He threatened me today. He said he
would have me put out of Dower House and
committed. He has the power, he says. Maybe
he does, but he wouldn't dare. The others don't
matter. They can be replaced. He can't replace
me. Without my cover he'd be lost. If anyone
else lived in Dower House it would all come
out. . . . He threatened me, but he won't do
anything to me. He hasn't got enough yet.
When he gets enough, I'll start to worry.

My aunt had been involved with the highwaymen. Somehow or other she had furnished cover
for them. I wondered how an old woman living
alone in an isolated house could do that. What
kind of cover could she give the thieves? Surely
they could not come and go at Dower House without being seen. It was a complete puzzle to me,
but as I read on the pieces of the puzzle began to
fit into place.

February 11th.   We were almost found out
last night. I had to think quick and lie convincingly in order to save the situation. One of the
farm women brought her daughter to see if I
had anything that would help the girl's cramps.
She had started cramping after supper and
when they didn't stop she brought the girl here.
It was after midnight and I had them both in
the kitchen. I had mixed up a powder and was
giving instructions on its use when we heard
something crash downstairs. This was followed
by voices. The women had been in the house

for half an hour. They were quite alarmed. I said the noises had come from the shed in back of the house. I told them I had given two Gypsies permission to sleep there for the night. I babbled on about how sound echoed so strangely this near the quarry, and I could see they were convinced, although the woman gave me a lecture about how dangerous Gypsies were. . . . They had knocked over a shelf of my best preserves.

The cellar! I had felt something wrong the first time I saw it. I remembered that horrid, fetid smell and that atmosphere of evil. No wonder I had reacted to it the way I had. They had been using the cellar for rendezvous. They probably met there. Perhaps they changed into their garb there. They could come to Dower House one by one, inconspicuously, without arousing any suspicion, but I wondered how they could all leave together without being seen. I thought about it, and I thought about the cellar, pressing my brows into a frown. There was another mystery here. In the back of my mind something was taunting me, as though a tiny voice I couldn't quite hear was trying to tell me the answers to all my questions.

The last entry in the notebooks caused me to shiver with horror. As I read it I suddenly knew the real reason why Roderick Mellory wanted me away from Dower House.

March 18th.   Feeling bad, very bad. Weak. I wonder. Of course he has tea with me, but I know all there is to know about poison. He is a devil, a devil, but he wouldn't do that. But he is very angry. Oh yes, he thought he was going to cheat me. He refused to give me my share, so I took it, took all I was entitled to. Almost half. He will never find it. No one will. He will have to start all over again, unless he listens to reason. He is coming here tonight. Perhaps we can strike a bargain. I am beginning to be a little afraid. I am his match, I know, but he was so incensed when he found I had taken the gold and hidden it. . . .

I closed the notebooks and sat there in the darkened room. All around me there was silence. A vein throbbed at my temple and my wrists felt weak. I thought about my aunt Lucille, a poor old woman whom I had never known. She had played a dangerous game with a dangerous man, and she had lost. She had double-crossed him. That had been a mistake. He had killed her for it. He would probably have killed her anyway. It gave me some satisfaction to know that she had outwitted him in at least one respect. How furious he must have been when he discovered that she had stolen from him in turn. Had he ever found the gold that she had hidden so skillfully?

The notebooks had been concealed in the secret drawer along with a revolver and a tarnished old key. I thought about that key. I wondered what lock it fit. I was suddenly quite anxious to find out.

13

*E*very drop of color had drainied out of the sky
as I drove Billy's wagon back to Dower House.
The road ahead was a dark gray ribbon, and the
trees were like grotesque black figures crowding
in on either side. There was no light left and the
stars had not yet appeared. Shadows thickened. A
brisk breeze stirred the grasses and rustled the
leaves overhead. Billy's gray moved at a brisk
trot, as eager to be home as I was. I clicked the
reins, urging him on.

I was strangely calm now, despite my hurry. All
the pieces of the puzzle seemed to fit together
nicely, and although it was not a pretty picture, it
gave me a strong sense of satisfaction to know
that any suspicions about Roderick Mellory had
been correct. He was the highwayman. He was
the man in black who had held up the coach that
brought me to Cornwall. Paul Mellory had told
me that his brother would stop at nothing to see
that Phoenix Hall was completely restored. How

true those words had been. Roderick Mellory had discovered a way to recoup the family fortune, and the fact that there was risk involved must have been a challenge to him.

It fit perfectly. He had the means. He had the position. He had an easy access to all private information. Being the Master of Phoenix Hall, he was above reproach. How he must have laughed as he deceived the people he detested, those innocent, naïve village officials who were all too ready to oblige the local aristocrat. My poor old aunt had somehow or other fallen in league with him. He could not very well use Phoenix Hall as a place of rendevous, so he talked my aunt into letting him use the cellar of Dower House. He could meet his cronies there without detection. He had promised the old woman a share of the plunder. When he failed to keep his promise she had stolen from him in turn, and he had killed her, just as he had killed the man whose body had been found in the ravine.

There had been no inquest when my aunt died. There had been no need for one. She was a very old woman who had apparently died a natural death. Only one man knew differently. No wonder Roderick Mellory wanted me out of Dower House. No wonder he had tried to frighten me away. Not only did I make it impossible for him to continue to use the place as a rendezvous, thus making his risks greater, but there was also a strong possibility that I might find some evidence of his crime.

He might have an even stronger motive still. I had no way of knowing that he had made a bargain with my aunt before killing her. I had no way of knowing that he had found the gold she had hidden. Perhaps it was still there. He had continued to stage the robberies after her death. Perhaps he had been trying to make up for what he had lost. It was ironic that he had been clever enough to deceive a whole county and yet had been unable to deceive an old woman. Because of her he would ultimately lose everything.

I did not doubt that my aunt had been senile. After losing her husband she had lived on all alone in the isolated house and that must have gradually worked on her mind. Everyone had called her eccentric. They had looked upon her with amused tolerance and some respect for her bizarre wisdom. She must have been a curious creature, serving as midwife by day and giving succor to thieves by night. Yet she had been shrewd. She had recorded all their transactions in her notebooks, and the notebooks would be proof enough to hang him.

Of course Greg knew. He had known the night of the ball. That probably explained his curious conduct, his extreme nervousness. He had decoded the notebooks and learned the truth about Roderick Mellory. He wanted to put the matter in the right hands, so he had contacted someone from London. The man who had brought a message at the ball was from Scotland Yard, not from the school. Greg had not gone back to Liverpool. He had gone back to London. They were preparing an airtight case against Roderick Mellory before they confronted him with the evidence. Perhaps they were even now spying on Phoenix Hall, waiting to catch him in some incriminating act. There was a big reward offered for the capture of the highwaymen. Greg would get that. It would be enough to enable him to leave the school and do as he wished.

I knew now why he had not told me any of this. It was a perfectly natural reaction on his part. He had not wanted to alarm me. Even in this he was thoughtful and considerate, the perfect gentleman. He had lied to me, true, but he had done so out of a sense of masculine protectiveness. And I had treated him so shabbily, I thought. I would make it up to him. As soon as this was all over with, I would make up for everything. I promised that as I drove towards home.

Night had completely fallen as I turned on the curve of road that led up to Dower House. A thin shell of moon had come out from behind the clouds and it shed mellow light. The roof of Dower House was washed with silver, but the walls were dark, the yard spread with shadows. No lights burned in any window. Nan and Billy had probably gone out for one of their amorous strolls and had not yet returned, and yet it was not like Nan to leave the house in darkness. Possibly they had gone out before dark.

I was a little alarmed as I stopped the wagon and climbed down. I had been gone longer than I had intended, of course, but still Nan should have cooked dinner. There should have been a light burning in the kitchen and the odors of food cooking. I stood there for a moment, my hand resting on the warm muzzle of Billy's dappled gray. The animal was placid, kicking his hooves lightly on the dirt. If anything were wrong he would have sensed it, I thought.

Then I wondered about Peter. He should be barking. He always rushed out to greet me when I had been gone. There was no sign of him now.

Well, I thought, perhaps they took him with them. I hesitated, looking at the dark house, and then I saw something far off, beyond the house. It lasted just a second, a brief flash, a tiny pinpoint of yellow light in the quarry behind Dower House. It came and went so quickly that I could not really be sure I had seen it.

I stepped across the yard and opened the front door, scolding myself for a too vivid imagination. Nan and Billy had gone for a walk. They were huddled together somewhere now, exchanging intimate confidences, and Peter was with them. A firefly had flashed in one of the shrubs, and I had let my imagination magnify it into a sinister light in the quarry. I should have better sense, I thought. I resolved to dress down Nan and Billy both for their thoughtlessness.

The house was very dark and still. I stood for a moment in the hall trying to get my bearings. I touched the wall and felt my way over to the little secretary where we kept matches. I opened the drawer and felt for the slender little sticks. My hand brushed over paper, ribbons, a package of seed, but I could not find the matches. We had probably used them all. I knew for certain that there were some in the parlor. I stumbled into the room, irritated with myself. It was so dark I could not feel a sense of direction.

I stood in the middle of the parlor. The curtains were drawn and not a drop of light penetrated into the room. Where was the desk? I started to move towards the right when I heard a noise that caused my pulses to leap. It was not my imagination this time. The noise was repeated, a rattle and creak that was here in the room with me. Someone was moving. The noise was followed by a faint chirp and I realized that Nan's canary had jumped up on his swing in the cage. The noise enabled me to find my bearings. I went to the desk and found the matches immediately.

The lamp spread a warm glow of light in the room. It was friendly and welcoming, all neat and clean as I had left it. The canary blinked sleepy eyes at me and hopped down from his swing to peck at his seed. I went into the kitchen and lit the lamp there. The room was filled with the fragrant odors of newly baked bread, and two golden brown loaves were setting on the drain board beside the whetstone and four newly sharpened knives. The light glittered on the long steel blades. Although Nan had cleaned up all of her bread making mess, there was a sprinkling of flour on the floor, and there were no signs of preparation for dinner.

I went back into the parlor and sat down, trying to curb my irritation with the negligent couple. This was not at all like Nan. I wondered if anything had happened. Had there been an accident? Had someone come to fetch Billy? Nan would have gone along with him if there promised to be any kind of excitement. There was bound to be any number of logical explanations for their absence, the most likely being the romantic stroll I had surmised in the first place. They were both young and carefree. What did a late dinner matter in the face of that?

The house was very quiet, almost too quiet. I could hear the wind in the trees outside, the limbs groaning. I could hear the clock ticking on the mantle. It was a monotonous sound, only emphasizing the silence. They would be back soon, surely. I did not like being alone. I had been upset by my discoveries, and I wanted to hear Nan's friendly chatter. I wanted to feel the security of Billy's presence. I sat there in the chair, my palms resting on the over-stuffed arms, waiting to hear the sound of footsteps on the gravel and Peter's excited yelp.

The clock ticked on. Merely sitting here only made matters worse. My impatience was getting out of bounds and I knew I could no longer wait. The key was in the desk drawer and I took it out, holding the tarnished object in the curve of my hand, examining it as though I had never seen a key before. If my aunt had hidden it in the secret drawer with the revolver and the notebooks, there must have been a reason. The key must have been important. I knew it did not fit any of the cabinets or drawers in the main part of the house. All those keys were on a ring I kept hanging beside the kitchen door. What could it possibly fit?

She had hidden the gold very skillfully. She would have put it somewhere where she could have more or less kept an eye on it. I did not think she would have buried it, and I was certain it was not stuffed away anywhere in the house. The key must be significant. It must have something to do with the hidden gold. Why else would she have put it away with the other things? I tried to think of any place I might have overlooked.

Then I remembered the cellar.

Of course. There were several old boxes and trunks down there. I had never gone through them. I had avoided the cellar whenever possible. The key must fit one of those locks. What a perfect place for the gold. Aunt Lucille had been a shrewd old woman, and she must have known her man very thoroughly. It was the one place he would not think to look. It was much too obvious. It was the one place he had most access to. The gold would be right there, within easy reach, and he would never have thought about looking for it right there under his eyes.

I grew more and more excited as I thought about this possibility. I grew convinced the gold was in the cellar. The cellar was the focal point of this whole afair, and if the gold was still at Dower House the cellar was the only place it could possibly be.

I had forgotten about Nan and Billy now. I had forgotten about everything else. I hurried into the kitchen and unlocked the door that led down to the cellar. A wave of cold, clammy air rustled up from the darkness and the fetid odor assailed my nostrils. I stood there, peering down. Something held me back. Perhaps it was the filth. Perhaps it was the smell. Perhaps it was the associations the place had in my mind. I could feel the clammy air on my arms, and the sour smell was ugly. It was a place of cobwebs and spiders and dust and darkness, and I hesitated. It would be much better to wait until morning. Then Billy could go down with me and I would not feel so uneasy.

I looked down at the key in my hand. It seemed to burn there in my palm, urging me to use it immediately. My curiosity got the better of me, overcoming the sense of uneasiness. I opened the cellar door all the way back and propped a chair against it to hold it open. It would be the first thing Nan and Billy would see when they came in. I took the oil lamp from the shelf and started down the stairs.

They were slick with moisture, and bits of

green moss grew between the cracks. The lamp spluttered, throwing garish shadows over the damp wall. It was very cold down here, and I shivered a little, standing at the foot of the stairs and wondering where to begin. A huge cobweb was draped over one corner, its silky threads dripping with moisture, and I shuddered as I saw a spider dangling in the center of the web. The earth floor was spongy to my feet. I set the lamp on a stack of old boxes and kneeled down before a small trunk.

It was not locked. It contained old photographs and ancient letters. I moved aside a basket of rubbish to get to a brassbound trunk that looked promising. It was locked securely, but the leather hinges were so old and mildewed that they broke easily and I was able to lift the lid. The trunk contained nothing but books.

The light flickered. I was extremely nervous. I kept looking over my shoulder as though I expected to see someone standing there in the shadows. I had the curious feeling that someone was watching me, but I knew it must be my imagination. There was a strange noise, too, a scurrying sound behind the shelves of poison. No doubt it was mice, but it worried me nevertheless. I was beginning to lose my nerve. I stood up, brushing the dirt from my skirt.

The oil lamp spilled a pool of spluttering light in the center of the room, but the rest of the cellar was in shadows. I held the lamp up, peering into the corners. I could not get over the feeling that a pair of eyes was fastened upon me. The sensation grew stronger. There was a crunching sound, like someone shifting his weight from one foot to the other. When I whirled around there was nothing but my own shadow on the wall. There was no one in the cellar besides myself. It was absurd to imagine these things, I told myself, trying to regain my composure. There was no possible way anyone could get here without coming down the steps, and the door had been securely locked. I moved the lamp to another stack of boxes so that it could illuminate another part of the cellar.

I was convinced that the gold was down here, or had been. The conviction grew stronger, and with it my determination to find a lock that would match the key. I knew I had seen other trunks here at one time or another. We had taken none of them upstairs. They must still be here. I saw an old dressmaker's dummy standing against the wall, the wire rusted, the padding coming out of the form. I paused, frowning. It should not have been there. It should have been in the corner, beside the wheelbarrow. That was where it had been the last time I was in the cellar. Then I noticed that several things were not where they had been before. Someone had moved them.

Nothing would induce Nan to come down here alone. Perhaps Billy had moved the things around, looking for some tool or other. Surely he had. I certainly hadn't. I frowned, bewildered. No one else could have done it. No one else could have been down here. It must have been Billy. But when had he been in the cellar recently to fetch something?

Then I saw the old brassbound trunk. It had been shoved against the wall. It was securely fastened with a heavy lock, and the lock was brass, green with tarnish. A stack of old newspapers and magazines was piled on top of the trunk. I pushed them aside and put the key into the lock. It went in smoothly, turned easily. The hinges creaked as I lifted the lid. A cloud of dust rose in my face and I coughed. The trunk was filled with balls of newspaper, tightly packed against four lumpy bags of worn chamois cloth. I took out one of the bags.

It was terribly heavy. It split open. Gold showered at my feet, and I let out a little cry. The gold glistened and glittered there on the floor of the cellar, all the brighter against the muddy surface. I looked at it with disbelief. It was hard to believe that it was really there, that I had actually discovered it.

So I had been right after all. I stared at the gold, frightened now. I did not want to touch it. I thought of all the hands that must have touched it, of all the crimes that had been committed for its sake. It was evil, and now that I had found it I merely wanted to run.

I heard the loud creaking noise. There was a sudden draft of cold air, sharp and chill, and the lamp fluttered wildly, throwing grotesque shadows on the wall. The wall that held the shelves of poison was swinging inwards, opening like a door. A jar of poison fell, shattered into a dozen pieces. I was paralyzed. I watched as the arm pushed the wall all the way back, and in the flickering light of the lamp I could see the man as he had been that other time, dressed all in black, a silky black hood over his head. He stood just inside the cellar.

"Thank you for finding it for me," he said. "I knew it must be here. I had been looking earlier."

"You?" I whispered.

"I knew it was in Dower House somewhere. That's why I wanted you to go away."

"You are the one," I said. My voice was barely audible.

He stepped fully into the cellar. Behind him I could see a long passage that led down into darkness. That explained so much. He had been here looking for the gold, and that explained the disorder. He had been here before, and I remembered the mysterious footprints I had found earlier. He had been standing behind the shelf of poison just now, watching me as I opened the lid of the trunk. He was a menacing figure as he moved towards me. The yellow light picked up the gloss on his tall black boots. I could see the butt of a revolver projecting from the belt of his tight black pants. The silky black hood completely covered his face, with only two holes at eye level. The eyes were watching me, waiting to see what I would do.

I stood up very straight, my back arched. I held my chin out, meeting his stare with calm eyes. Only my hands betrayed me. They trembled visibly, and I put them behind me, hoping that he had not noticed.

"You are the one who tried to frighten me away," I said. "You threw the rock with the warning note tied to it."

"I had one of my men do it, Angela."

"Why? Why did you want to frighten me?"

"I wanted you out of the way."

"You knew the gold was here?"

"I suspected it. I knew it couldn't be far away. I didn't think of the cellar until I read the notebooks."

"I went to the school this afternoon. I found them."

"Pity," he said. "I had hoped I could pull all this

off without involving you. I hoped I could get the gold and then persuade you to leave with me. I've been back to Liverpool. I've booked passage on a ship sailing for South America. Everything is ready. I even have passports for a Mr. Andrews and his wife."

"You thought I would go with you?"

He nodded. The eyes did not leave my face.

"You were wrong, Greg."

"I think not," he said.

"The night of the ball—" I began. "There was no sick child. There was no message from the school."

"That fool Clements. He came. He was panicky. We were almost caught after the last robbery. They searched the quarry and passed right by the crevice that leads to the cave. This passage connects with the cave. All the rest of the loot is there, and the clothes. Clements came to Phoenix Hall. He was drunk. He demanded his part of the gold. He wanted to take it and leave for Devon and be done with it."

"So you killed him."

"I had no choice."

"I saw his body in the ravine."

"I'm sorry about that, Angela. I had hoped to spare you any of the ugliness."

"You killed my aunt, too."

"I had to do it. She refused to cooperate. She was an old fool. We had a good thing going, and she wanted to spoil it. It was not a painful death. The poison worked like a sleeping tablet and she felt nothing. No one suspected anything."

"How much did she know?"

"Everything. She is the one who first showed me this passage. It was perfect for my purposes.

The cave was a perfect hideout, and I saw how I could work out the whole thing. She thought I was joking at first, but after the first attack when she saw the gold she was ready to help me in any way she could."

He stood there a few feet from me, his fists resting on his hips. He spoke in a calm, level voice, objectively, as though he were explaining some point in a lesson to his students. I began to back away slowly, and he shook his head warningly, taking another step towards me.

"Why did you do it, Greg?" I asked, my voice beginning to tremble.

"It was a challenge," he said. "I wanted to get away. I wanted to escape this monotonous existence and live like I was intended to live, and I needed money in order to do that, a lot of money. After the first attack I saw how incredibly simple it was. I decided to get enough to live like I wanted to live for the rest of my life. I saw how stupid they all were, how trusting and vulnerable, and it was a pleasure to make fools of them. No one ever suspected the proper Mr. Ingram. I even helped them chart out new routes that would deceive the highwaymen."

I could see how pleased he was with himself. I could see how his ego had been fed by his exploits. This man was completely different from the one I had known. He was cold-blooded. He was dangerous. He had no sense of right and wrong. I knew that he could kill me just as easily as he had killed my aunt and that he would feel no remorse for it.

"And then I came to Dower House," I said.

"Yes, you came. You were an obstacle."

"So you tried to frighten me away."

"I did not want you to be hurt. I did not want you to be involved. I wanted to spare you."

"And now?"

"And now Mr. and Mrs. Andrews will sail for South America. It will be wonderful there, Angela. I'll buy a plantation. We'll live like royalty and never want for anything."

"I won't go with you, Greg. You must know that."

"Are you quite certain?" His voice was cold and flat.

I nodded. My throat was dry. I couldn't speak.

"Then I will have to kill you, Angela. That will be a pity. I meant all those things I said."

He shrugged his shoulders as though this was all very distasteful to him. The hand in the black glove moved slowly down to his belt, the fingers resting on the butt of the revolver. My blood felt icy cold. My wrists were limp and a vein throbbed at my temple. He pulled the revolver out slowly, holding it in the palm of his hand and looking down at it. It was long and black. He spun the cartridge chamber with his thumb. It made a deadly clicking sound.

"I'm sorry about this," he said, his voice still level. "It seems the only alternative."

I was standing beside the stack of boxes on which the lamp set. They were piled precariously, and the lamp was perched near the edge of the top box. The flame danced nimbly in the draft of air coming from the passage.

He stopped playing with the revolver. His fingers tightened on the butt, and he pointed the weapon towards me. I could see his eyes through the holes in the black hood. They were calm, undisturbed. I looked down at the long barrel aimed

at my breast, and then I kicked the bottom box.
The stack tilted violently and the lamp flew to the
floor. The light spluttered out in one last explosion of yellow, and the cellar was in total darkness.

"That was a foolish trick," he said. "I expected
more dignity from you, Angela."

I stood quietly for a moment. I was certain he
could hear my heart beating. I began to move
cautiously towards the stairs. I knew exactly
where they were. I had hastily gained a sense of
direction as the last light fluttered out. There was
a barrel in the way, and I moved around it, touching the rim lightly with my fingertips. A box of
bulbs set in the path. I stepped over it. Greg did
not move. I could sense his presence. I could feel
his cold anger. My foot touched the slimy surface
of the bottom step. I laid my hand on the wall for
support. I moved quickly, too quickly. I was half-
way up the steps when my feet slid out from under me. I fell, sprawled out over the steps. He
laughed quietly, and then I heard the rasping
scratch as he struck a match.

He found the lamp. It had not broken. Not all
of the oil had spilled out. He set it on the boxes.
The first match burned out. He struck another. I
saw him bending over the lamp, very carefully
lighting the wick. I could not move. I was paralyzed with fear. I watched him with horrified fascination, as those condemned must watch their
executioners making final preparations. He stood
for a moment, rubbing his gloved hands together
as the wick flared and the glow of light began to
spread. His back was to me. He was bent over a
little, his legs planted wide apart. I saw his broad
shoulders covered in black, the folds of the hood

hanging loosely from his head. He stood up straight and turned towards me, reaching for the revolver which he had laid aside.

He moved slowly towards the steps. He seemed bored with all this, as though it were merely a tedious detail that he had to take care of. He came to the foot of the stairs and stood there, looking up at me. I could hear nothing but my own heart pounding. I clasped my lower lip between my teeth and bit down, staring at the man who held the revolver on me. Then I saw that he was looking beyond me, at some point above my head. He raised the revolver. I heard the explosion and saw the silver-blue flash streaking the air. Greg stood for a moment with the gun still raised, and then he fell against the wall, crumpling into a heap as the life went out of him.

Roderick Mellory was standing at the head of the stairs. He did not look at the man he had killed. He looked at me. One eyebrow was raised in a caustic arch, and his lips were pressed tightly together. The revolver in his hand was still smoking.

14

*T*he morning was lovely, far too lovely to be endured indoors. I sat in the garden, a book of poetry unopened in my lap. The sky was white, with just a touch of blue, and billowing white clouds moved lazily over its surface. The larkspurs were blooming profusely, the blue petals curving out towards the sun. Billy had edged the bed with crushed white shell, and the pattern of blue and white was serene. Peter curled at my feet, a huge mound of sleek silver fur, breathing contentedly. I wore a dress of white cotton with a tiny pattern of blue and violet, and a violet ribbon held my hair back. The sun touched my eyelids, making me drowsy.

From the house came the cheerful sounds of Nan supervising the men who were cleaning out the cellar. They brought up armloads of rubbish. We would have a huge bonfire later on and I would be glad to see most of the things go up in flames. The secret passage had been sealed off.

The constable had found the cache where the rest of the gold had been hidden, and he had found evidence that had helped him locate and arrest the other men who had been involved. It was all over, all the hideous questioning, all the documents to sign and official statements to make. I wondered how I had been able to endure the nervous tension of it all.

I had seen Roderick Mellory only once. He had been in the office while I was answering questions for the men from Scotland Yard, and he had looked bored with the whole affair. When it came his turn to answer questions, he did so in a cold, condescending manner that put the men off considerably. He had not looked at me once, and my cheeks had flushed with embarrassment during the whole ordeal. When it was over he had left without so much as a word to me and extreme irritation had taken the place of embarrassment.

I owed my life to Roderick Mellory. That irritated me, too. I did not want to be obligated to him for anything. Why couldn't it have been someone else standing there at the head of the stairs with a smoking revolver? Nan had told me how she and Billy had become worried when I did not return from town in time for dinner. Nan thought I might have stopped at Phoenix Hall to visit with Laurel for a while, and they had gone there. When Roderick Mellory learned what had happened he began a search immediately. They were in the quarry when I returned, and I had seen their light. When they saw the light come on in Dower House, they had returned. It had taken them quite a while as they had been on the other side of the quarry. I shuddered to think what might have happened had they been a few minutes later.

That had all been over a week ago, and now I merely wanted to try and forget it. It would not be easy, I knew that. This exorcism of the cellar would help. I saw Billy go round the side of the house, his arms laden with old boxes. Nan followed him, an apron tied round her waist, a cap perched precariously on her golden curls. She waved a feather duster and yelled for him to be sure and put the trash in the pile behind the shed. Two other men followed them, one carrying the old dressmaker's dummy. I turned my attention back to the book of poetry, trying to concentrate on the lines.

I had not heard the horse coming up the road. When I looked up Roderick Mellory was dismounting. He wore glossy black boots, tight dove gray pants and a brown suede jacket with brown velvet lapels. There was a fawn colored ascot at his throat, and his raven black hair was disarrayed by the ride, a lustrous tangle that fell about his forehead. He carried a leather riding crop, slapping it against his boot as he walked towards me. He looked grim and determined, his lips pressed down at the corners.

I stood up, meeting his gaze with a haughty stare of my own.

"How is our heroine this morning?" he asked.

I frowned at his use of the dramatic word. "Just fine," I snapped.

"In fine spirits, at least," he said.

"What do you want, Mr. Mellory?" I asked. My voice was frigid.

"I am the man who saved your life," he said

lightly. "Do you really think that tone is appropriate, Miss Todd?"

"I suppose I should thank you for that," I said.

He made a mocking little bow, nodding his head and slapping the crop smartly against the side of his boot. I stood waiting, all my defenses set against the man. He grinned at me, and I could feel the flush coloring my cheeks. That irritated me, and I turned away quickly, hoping that he had not seen. He laughed quietly, still slapping the crop against his boot. I felt humiliated that he had made me blush, that he even had the power to make me blush.

"Have you decided to sell Dower House to me?" he asked.

I faced him, disdainful of flushed cheeks now. "Of course not! You may as well give up, Mr. Mellory. There is no way you can get it. It is mine, and I intend to keep it."

"There is one way," he said. There was a lilt in his voice.

"Really?"

"Yes."

"And how is that?" I asked.

"I could marry the mistress of Dower House. Then it would be mine."

"What an absurd idea, Mr. Mellory."

"Do you think so?"

"Completely absurd."

"I think not," Roderick Mellory said.